ABOUT THE AUTHOR

Dionne Haynes spent most of her childhood in Plymouth, England. She graduated from medical school in London and enjoyed a career as a doctor for over twenty years. After returning to Plymouth, she traded medicine for a career writing historical fiction.

BY DIONNE HAYNES

The Second Mrs Thistlewood

The Roseland Collection
Mawde of Roseland
Mistress of Carrick

The Mayflower Collection
Winds of Change
Running With The Wind
The Winter Years
The Trelawney Girl

For more information and updates:
www.dionnehaynes.com

THE TRELAWNEY GIRL

DIONNE HAYNES

Published by Allium Books 2025
22 Victoria Road, St Austell, Cornwall, PL25 4QD

Copyright © Dionne Haynes 2025

First published by Allium Books in 2025
Allium Books is a publishing imprint for
Dionne Haynes, Author

A CIP catalogue record for this book is available from the
British Library

Paperback ISBN: 978-1-915696-08-3
Ebook ISBN: 978-1-915696-09-0

Cover design by Dee Dee Book Covers

For my dearest friends who are like family to me.
They know who they are.

CHAPTER 1

Hester moved among the wedding guests, taking care not to catch her walking stick on a skirt hem or a shoe. A few guests enquired about her well-being. Others smiled before turning away to resume conversations with family members or friends. Hester found it hard to be civil and longed to go home, but Ma and Pa were deep in conversation with John and Priscilla Alden, and her brother and sister were nowhere to be seen.

The beat of a drum signalled the start of another round of dancing. Hester perched on a bench at the side of the barn and watched young men invite young women to take their hands and move around the floor in time with the music. The women blushed as they interlocked fingers with the eligible young men of the colony – young men a few of the women had set their hearts on marrying. Hester's gaze drifted to her cumbersome boots. The tired leather was scruffy and resembled something her father would wear for digging up vegetables from their garden or making repairs to their house. Never had she hated them so much.

As the dancing picked up pace, the air in the barn turned oppressive, heavy with the odours of greasy tallow candles, spilt Bride Ale and sweating bodies. The old barn was far too small for the large number of wedding guests, but the heat of the August day had given way to a deluge of rain that had driven them all indoors. Hester tipped her chin towards her chest and watched a rapid parade of colourful leather shoes. Ribbons and buckles threatened to work loose as wooden heels pounded to the beat and scuffed against the compacted earthen floor.

'Dance with me?' Little Ruth Alden engaged Hester with wide, pleading eyes. 'My brothers said they would, but I can't find them anywhere!' Ruth pressed her hands against Hester's legs and bounced on her toes. 'Please dance, Hester. Please!'

The dancing had already continued for longer than Hester had expected. Such a rowdy celebration rebelled against the stifling Puritan rules that had swept through the colony during the previous ten years. But the barn was on private Alden land, well out of earshot of its neighbours. It was unlikely to attract unwelcome attention, and the celebrations looked set to continue late into the night. The beat of the tabor caused a thrumming in Hester's head, and the screech of a fiddle prickled at the roots of her hair. Her mother and father swept past in a blur of orange and blue. Her mother's delighted tinkling laugh made Hester clench her jaw. She forced herself to smile at the sweet little girl jiggling up and down in front of her. Ruth was the only person in the barn who had asked Hester to dance.

'I can't, Ruth. You must ask someone else.'

'Why not?' Ruth's eyes narrowed into a frown. Her bottom lip pouted.

Hester scanned the seething mass of men and women moving in concentric circles, bobbing and dipping in time with the tune of an overexuberant fiddle. 'I'm sorry, Ruth, I just can't.'

Hester's deformed left foot throbbed inside her reinforced boot, and she felt the hot sting of a blister bubbling under her skin. She had slipped on a wet patch of deck during the short voyage from Plimoth, and her swollen skin had rubbed against the boot leather during the walk from Duxbury to the Alden farmstead.

Ruth gave a dramatic sigh and turned to face the dancers. 'I hope I look as pretty as my sister when I marry,' she said, wriggling onto the bench beside Hester.

Hester turned her gaze towards the bride. Wearing a bright yellow kirtle, Elizabeth Alden looked radiant. A coronet of delicate phlox flowers shimmered against her dark hair, and her flushed face glowed with joy. Hester watched Elizabeth glance towards her handsome new husband, and she caught the looks of adoration that passed between them. She pressed her lips together and swallowed. She did not begrudge Elizabeth the joy of finding love but simmered in the disappointment that such happiness would never be hers. No man ever desired a woman with a club foot, a woman who drew murmurs of pity as she limped about the neighbourhood.

Hester eased herself off the bench and took Ruth's clammy hand in hers. 'Come, let us find my sister. Martha will dance with you.'

Martha was in the outermost ring, the steps of the dance sweeping her towards them. When she drew level, Hester tapped her shoulder and held Ruth's hand towards her. Martha acknowledged Ruth with a smile and grasped the little girl's fingers. Hester waited for them to move away, then discreetly slipped outdoors.

Puddles glistened in the moonlight. Stars glittered against a grey-blue sky. A dog barked in the distance, and crickets chirruped nearby. The air tasted sweet on Hester's lips, freshly cleansed by the rain.

Hester's stick sent up tiny splashes with every strike of the ground. Her heavy boots sloshed across a rain-soaked track leading towards the town. She slipped into a grave-yard and sat down on a patch of wet mossy grass, her skirts puddling out around her and drawing moisture into the wool. After loosening the lace of her left boot, she eased it off her foot, taking a sharp intake of breath as the leather dragged against a large blister. Her grey stocking seemed to glow where it covered her misshapen ankle, and a large hole had appeared where it had rubbed against her boot. She smacked the ground, brushing the edge of her hand against the withering petals of a posy nestling at the foot of a grave marker. She traced the lettering on the cool, damp wood and murmured a heartfelt apology. It marked the burial place of a young woman from Duxbury.

Hester had known the woman well – she had helped Ma deliver her last two children. The small posy must have been left by one of the woman's four daughters. *How awful*, Hester thought, *to lose one's mother whilst so young.*

A squeak of a gate and rustling footsteps drew her attention away from the grave. She strained to make out the moving shape beside the furthest wall. It was the silhouette of an amorous couple locked in an embrace – a private lovers' tryst. Hester balled her skirt in her fists and clenched the fabric until her knuckles hurt. She choked on a wave of loneliness and let out a stifled sob. It seemed that no matter where she went, she felt like she did not belong. It was a pervading sense of displacement, a feeling she could not explain. The shadows in the distance giggled before moving deeper into the gloom, leaving Hester to rue the fact that romance would never come her way. Not for her an attentive admirer or a devoted husband like Pa. Not for her a cheeky little son nor a sweet little daughter like Ruth.

Hester forced her foot back into her boot, smarting as the leather chafed against raw skin. She closed her eyelids until the burning pain subsided and then, with a final glance towards the secret lovers, she reached for her walking stick. Suppressing the urge to cry out in pain, Hester pushed herself up to stand. It was time to cast her dreams aside and accept that she was imperfect. She must resign herself to a spinster's life and her future as a midwife.

CHAPTER 2

MEN, women and children climbed the hill to the fort, beckoned to the Sabbath service by the sound of a beating drum. Hester watched them from the bottom of the slope and leaned heavily on her stick. She pictured them filling the meeting room, settling on benches and clutching their psalters while waiting for the sermon to begin. When the doors closed and the drum fell silent, Hester turned to face the sea. The harbour was empty apart from a scattering of fishing boats lying at anchor and a small skiff tied up alongside the wooden pier. Gentle waves lapped the shore, caressing the sand and shingle. A large cormorant emerged from the shallows and settled on a boulder, stretching its glossy wings to dry the feathers in the late September sunlight.

Hester drew a deep lungful of cool autumnal air and tasted salt on her lips. She had made excuses to avoid attending each Sabbath service of late. The recent wedding in Duxbury had caused a nuptial fever, and there was too much talk about marriages planned for the following spring. Even Hester's closest friends shared their hopes of finding husbands, but Hester did not dare to dream of losing her heart to a young man. There seemed little point. She gazed towards the horizon and her thoughts drifted to London. She wondered if life was better there, if it was easier than in New England. Hester had been born in London and wished she had memories of her life there, but Ma and Pa had brought her to Plimoth when she was only two or three.

'I see I'm not the only person to avoid the sermon this morning.' The velvety voice of the blacksmith's son jolted Hester out of her reverie.

'Master Phillips. Good morrow to you.' Hester's words sounded brittle as her tongue seemed to stiffen and dry. Heat flooded her cheeks.

'We are friends, Hester, are we not? I beg you to drop the formality and address me by my name.'

Hester inclined her head a little and snuck a peek at her striking companion. Hundreds of tiny freckles dotted his creamy skin and a gentle breeze ruffled his unruly orange curls. His clean-shaven face gave him a boyish look, much younger than his twenty-two years. He held a felt hat in his right hand and a small leather pouch in his left. He stowed the leather pouch inside his jerkin while continuing to look at Hester. His eyes sparkled with joy and his thin lips were parted into the kindest of smiles. They had known each other since childhood, but now Adam was a grown man and Hester a young woman.

'Well?'

'Yes, we are most certainly friends. Good morrow to you, Adam.'

'And a good morrow to you too, Hester.' Adam jerked his head towards the hill leading to the fort. 'Were you not in the mood for praising our Lord today?'

'I give my thanks to our Lord and praise Him every morning when I wake and several times during each day. He'll forgive me for not wanting to climb the hill to praise Him whilst I am out of sorts.'

'Forgive me, Hester, I did not mean to be flippant.' Adam's expression turned solemn. 'I should have known you'd have a good reason. Is the pain severe today?'

'No worse than usual, and there are people suffering more than I am. What's your excuse for missing the sermon?'

'My father and I were late home from Boston. A problem with a wheel on our cart left us camping under the stars last night. We arrived home a few minutes ago. I saw you standing here staring out to sea and thought I might join you for a short while.'

'I'm glad of your company.' Hester straightened her posture. 'Tell me, Adam, do you ever wonder if you shouldn't be here?'

Adam puckered his brow. 'Goodness, that's something I've never considered. Why do you ask?'

'I don't know.' Hester spent a few moments trying to find the right words. 'It's as if I'm watching people go about their business, moving around me, talking to each other. I can see them and hear them, and they can see me, but for a reason I cannot fathom, I don't feel part of their world.' Hester watched the cormorant dive back into the water. When it emerged, it had a small fish clamped in its beak. 'It's possible it's because of something my mother said several weeks ago. She had a dear friend we used to visit, an indigenous woman named Weetamoo.' Hester cast her mind back to when she was ten years old. Happy memories flooded into her mind. 'Oh, how I loved it when Ma used to take me to Weetamoo's village! Weetamoo called me "The Chosen One". I don't know why she called me that. I think it was because she would sit with me and tell me about her ancestors while teaching me some of her native ways, like how to weave coloured baskets or make beads from shells. She never did that with Martha.'

'You don't see her any more?' Adam asked.

Hester shook her head. 'We haven't seen Weetamoo or her family for five or six years.' She lowered her voice. 'Not since the smallpox came over from Europe and killed many of her people. Ma said that was part of the reason that tension is building here. She said they regret allowing us to settle because it no longer feels like their homeland. Ma fears that one day it could lead to bloodshed.'

'Your mother may well be right.' Adam rubbed at a small black mark that stained the brim of his hat. 'It's bad enough hearing reports about the Civil War in England. Too many men lose their lives in battles because of disagreements about how things should be.'

The sky darkened. Thunder rumbled in the distance. Cold raindrops struck Hester's face and hands. She raised the hood of her woollen cape to cover her linen coif. 'I fear we're in for a drenching if we stay here much longer. I must bid you a good day, Adam Phillips.'

Adam pushed his hat onto his head. 'And I will bid you a good day too, Hester, but first, I will escort you to your home.'

CHAPTER 3

'THE HUMILIATION OF IT!' Martha stomped into the house, and Ma's pewter serving plates rattled on the dresser as the door slammed behind her. 'Look at this!' Martha brandished a dirty shoe at Hester. The leather upper had come away from the sole leaving the edge too ragged to be restitched. 'I swear everyone was laughing at me as I walked home from the service. I slipped twice and scraped my hand on a wall when I reached out to save myself.' She threw the broken shoe into the corner of the room and grimaced at her grazed palm.

Hester observed the filth clinging to Martha's stocking. Beneath the layers of mud and wool, her sister's foot was dainty and she had neat little toes. She pictured her own feet, buried within her boots. Her right foot was normal enough, but her left foot was unsightly. It tended to droop and twist inward, and thick calluses had formed on her skin from rubbing against metal supports concealed within the stiff leather seams of her boots.

Ma retrieved Martha's broken shoe from the floor and

turned it over in her hand. 'This is beyond repair, Martha. I'm afraid you'll have to make do with your clogs until we see the cordwainer for a new pair.'

'Do you think I'll have new shoes before the next Sabbath service?'

'No, Martha, I don't. You may borrow a pair of my shoes for the Sabbath, but otherwise it's clogs.'

'But Ma, imagine what my friends will say if I dress like a pauper!'

Hester harrumphed. 'I doubt they'll even notice.' Hester would happily settle for clogs if only she could wear them! 'May I have a new pair of boots, Ma?' She pointed to a worn patch of leather on her left boot, near the stitching to the sole. 'I fear this might break down any day and leave me no better off than Martha.'

'No, Hester.' Ma had a sharp edge to her voice. 'You must wait a little longer. We all need new linens, and your father wants a new jerkin. Lord knows, we would have everything we need if only he would press his patients for payment.'

'But Ma, if my boot breaks down, I won't be able to leave the house!'

A flicker of irritation crossed her mother's brow. 'I said no, Hester. Martha's shoe is beyond repair so she cannot wear it, but your boot leather has life in it yet.' Ma beckoned to Martha. 'Come to the stillroom with me. I'll apply a salve to your injured hand.'

Chastened, Hester hobbled across the room and settled on a chair by the fire. 'Surely Martha can put up with wearing clogs!' she muttered, glaring at the flames. She fiddled with a loose thread on her skirt but pulled on the thread a little too firmly and caused a small hole to appear. She clenched her jaw. It was another piece of clothing she would have to repair. She pulled the thread harder and watched the hole grow bigger. If the leather ripped on her boot like that, she would have no support for her foot. It would leave her trapped at home while her mother went out to deliver babies without her, and Hester would never become a competent midwife if her mother did all the work.

A flash of lightning was soon followed by a loud rumble of thunder. Raindrops pattered against the glass with the start of another heavy downpour. Hester heard Pa call Samuel's name from somewhere beyond the window. Pounding footsteps approached the house and then the door was flung open. Pa stumbled into the house with Samuel close behind him. They slipped off their mud-coated boots and hung their sodden winter cloaks on hooks. The musty odour of wet wool wafted across the room while rainwater pooled on the floorboards.

'Who fancies a game of merels?' Pa said. A drop of water fell from his hair and trickled along his nose. He swept it away with the back of his hand and ran his fingers through his hair. Fine droplets sprayed around him, dotting the plaster on the wall.

'I'll play you, Pa.' Hester reached across to a shelf and grasped a carved wooden board worn smooth with use and a small box containing the merel counters.

'After me!' Samuel snatched the box and board from Hester's hands.

'Samuel!' Hester chided. 'I said I would play first.'

Samuel gave a nonchalant shrug. 'I have the board and counters,' he said, rattling the merels.

'I'll play one game with Sam, Hester, then it will be your turn.' Pa sat in his chair at the head of the table and stacked his counters in a neat pile.

'Or perhaps you and I could play chess, Pa?'

Pa was always so busy during the day attending to his patients, and Hester was never as good as her siblings at getting his attention when he returned home late in the evenings. A game of chess would take longer than merels and buy her the time with him she yearned for. And chess was Pa's favourite game.

'Chess it is,' Pa said, gesturing for Sam to take the first turn at their game of merels. 'Desire, did I tell you I saw John Alden yesterday?' Pa said when Ma returned to the room. 'He was with their eldest boy. What a close likeness they share! Joseph has his father's lips and nose and even shares his passion for whittling.'

Ma reached her hand towards Samuel's head and ruffled the seven-year-old's hair. 'Your son bears a striking resemblance to you, Jed. Look at how he narrows his eyes and purses his lips while he decides where to place his counter. That's the same expression you have when studying your case notes.'

'Do children always resemble their parents?' Hester asked, looking at Ma and wondering what similarities they might share.

'Not always, but there's often something about a child that resembles one of their parents.' Ma tipped her head to one side. 'Come to think of it, all of John and Scilla's children bear a resemblance to one another.' She chuckled. 'They all have John's nose.'

Hester ran her fingertip along the contours of her own nose. There was a slight bump just below the bridge, and the tip was flat, as if she had held it pressed against a window for far too long. Ma's nose was straight and elegant, although it tended to bleed.

Pa and Samuel fell silent, concentrating on their game. Ma sat at the table with them and opened her delivery ledger to peruse her notes about the expectant mothers that would soon go into labour. Martha settled on a chair opposite Hester with a book open on her lap. As she lost herself in its pages, her left hand reached for a lock of hair, and she twirled it around her index finger. Hester's gaze drifted from Martha to Ma. She too was twirling a lock of hair while studying entries in her ledger. Hester slipped off her coif, freeing her hair and sending it tumbling across her shoulders. She copied her mother and sister by wrapping a lock around her finger, but the action felt unnatural and made her arm muscles ache. Hester pushed herself up from her chair. She would rather watch a slow game of merels than mimic Ma and Martha.

CHAPTER 4

LATE THE FOLLOWING EVENING, there was a frantic knocking at the door. The latch lifted and the hinges creaked as it opened moments later. Francis Billington peered inside.

'Mistress Trelawney? Forgive me for intruding, but my wife needs you.'

'Come in out of the rain, Francis.' Ma rose from her seat and hurried towards him. 'Is she in labour?'

Francis nodded, tipping a thin trickle of rainwater from the brim of his hat. His face was pale; his lips were set in a thin line.

Hester put her needlework aside and pushed herself up from her chair. It was clear from the fear in Francis's eyes that he had cause for concern.

'How long has she been labouring?' Ma asked Francis as she threw an oiled cape around her shoulders.

'Since midday, I believe, but the pain's been bad since sundown.' Francis hesitated. 'I said I'd fetch one of our neighbours, but Christian was adamant I should come for you. She said to tell you she fears the baby is stuck.'

'I'll go with you,' Hester said, grabbing her walking stick and Ma's delivery bag. She had witnessed a few difficult births, but not one where the child was stuck. This was an important opportunity to learn, and she was not willing to miss it. 'You might need me to assist.'

'Thank you, Hester.' Ma grabbed another oiled cape and passed it to Hester. 'It's a foul night for going out, but such is the life of a midwife.'

Heavy rain pelted the street, sending muddy splashes across the threshold and into the house. Francis Billington's home was several streets away, and time was of the essence.

Hester glanced into the stormy night. 'You go on, Ma. I'll catch up with you as fast as I can.' *Dear Lord*, she said in a silent prayer, *don't let my boots break apart tonight*.

Pa approached with two lanterns made from tin and cow horn. He gave one to Ma. 'Don't worry, Desire, I'll escort Hester. Martha can play merels with Samuel until I return.'

When Hester and Da reached the Billington home, they found the children huddled in a corner of the parlour. Their pale faces shone through the gloom, made eerie by the flickering flames of smoking tallow candles. A gust of wind rattled the shutters, and the door slammed behind Hester. One of the little girls let out a shriek. The oldest sister drew her closer, murmuring words of reassurance. Francis Billington did not seem to hear. He continued pacing back and forth, running his fingers through his hair and muttering to himself.

'Join your mother,' Pa said, helping Hester out of her cape. 'I'll calm Francis before I head home.'

A shrill cry drew Hester towards the bedchamber.

Ma promptly vacated a low stool positioned at the foot of the bed and instructed Hester to sit on it. 'You deliver this,' she said. 'The head is already crowning.'

'Your baby is almost here, Christian,' Hester said in a calm, controlled voice. 'Stop pushing now, otherwise you'll tear. Try to take a few steady breaths.'

'I'd forgotten how much it hurts,' Christian said through gritted teeth.

'You'll forget again soon enough.' Hester rested her palm on Christian's belly and felt her womb tighten as a strong contraction took hold. 'Quick breaths now, Christian.' She watched the skin stretch open around the baby's head. 'That's it, nice and steady. I don't want you to rip.'

The baby's head emerged, and Hester swept her finger around its neck. 'Cord,' she whispered as her mouth turned dry. She tried to slip the loop of cord over the baby's head, but the loop was tight. Sweat pricked at her armpits. She tried a second time, but the cord would not shift.

'I want to push,' Christian said.

'Not yet,' Hester said, trying to stay calm. 'Thread,' she said to Ma.

Ma was ready with two lengths of thread and passed one to Hester. Hester held her breath. She fought to pass the thread between the cord and the baby's neck. At last, she had both pieces of thread secured with tight knots. She snipped the cord between them and took a gasping breath.

'Now you can push,' Hester said, throwing Ma a smile of relief.

With two more pushes, the baby's body emerged.

'He's a large baby, Christian,' Hester said, as she checked the baby's mouth, fingers and toes. 'No wonder it was a struggle to push him out.' She wrapped the baby in a sheet and admired his dark shock of hair and plump little lips. The baby let out a loud wail. Hester handed him to Christian. 'He wants his mother,' she said.

Hester left Ma to wash Christian and dress her in a clean shift while Hester separated the sheets that would launder well from those that needed burning. Once she was happy that the room was tidy and Christian looked presentable, she opened the door to announce that all was well following the little boy's delivery. The children filed into the small bedchamber, each one smiling as they took up positions alongside Christian's bed. Francis stood behind them, glowing with joy and pride. Hester looked at each child's face. They shared their father's dimples and his glittering blue eyes.

'What will you name this child, Francis?' Ma asked.

'Isaac,' Francis replied.

'May he bring joy and laughter befitting of his name,' Hester said, smiling at Francis. She pointed to the bundle of soiled linens. 'They're ready for the fire,' she said.

'I'll burn them outside in the morning,' Francis replied.

With one more glance towards Christian and her baby, Hester said, 'My mother and I will leave you now. You know where we are if you need us.'

Ma patted Francis's arm. 'Your children look so much like you, and no doubt Isaac will too.'

Francis beamed at Ma. "Tis a blessing when our children share our likeness.' He threw Hester a fleeting glance, and his smile faded. She thought she saw pity in his eyes. Pity directed at her.

Hester's appetite deserted her for most of the following day. At suppertime, she forced herself to eat and managed a few mouthfuls of bread and honey washed down with sips of ale. She helped Martha clear the table, then topped up Ma's soothing oils. She added them to the delivery bag along with a pile of laundered cloths. Next, she scraped the scissors clean and sharpened the blades with a small abrasive stone. With all her chores finished for the evening, she took a candle to the table and settled to read her favourite book: an English translation of a Spanish tale about a knight named Don Quixote. Usually, Hester would stifle her chuckles at the knight's comical antics, but this evening her concentration wandered, blurring the illustrations and words. Her gaze drifted to her sister. Martha was sitting by the hearth, repairing a tear in one of Pa's shirts. She had removed her coif, and her long dark locks glistened in the firelight. Hester envied her sister's hair. It was thick and lustrous like Ma's, while her own was fine and a dull shade of brown. Even her brother had glossier hair than she did.

Martha looked up from her needlework and glared at Hester. 'You're staring at me. Stop it at once!'

'I'm not staring, Martha,' Hester said, resisting the urge to snap back. 'I'm simply observing you.'

'And why would you want to do that?' Martha tutted and furrowed her brow before returning her attention to her stitches.

'Forgive me, Martha. I meant no offence.'

Martha's angry face soon relaxed, and she hummed a tune to herself. Her long slender fingers darted back and forth with the needle and thread.

Hester forced herself to study the open page of her book. Don Quixote was charging his horse towards a windmill, sword raised high as if he might strike at the windmill's sails. She clamped a piece of the inside of her cheek between her teeth, struggling to contain her tears. Martha had so many of Ma's best features. Not only her hair and her rosebud mouth, but her graceful movements and velvety singing voice.

Hester pushed herself up from the table and lit a fresh candle. She made her way up the stairs and into her parents' bedchamber. She opened a large casket in which Ma kept her special trinkets and took out a small mirror with silver filigree edging. It was a trinket Hester had adored since she was a little girl. The silver had turned dark grey and felt cool against her skin. The glass had mottled over the years and had a small crack near the top that distorted part of her reflection.

Hester removed her cap and shook out her hair. She raised the mirror and inspected her reflection for a feature resembling Ma, hoping for a resemblance Martha did not share. She scrutinised her pale skin and the angle of her nose, then watched the shallow lift in her cheeks as she forced her thin lips into a smile. She traced the tiny creases by her dark brown eyes and scowled at the widow's peak that distorted her hairline. Next, she forced a tinkling laugh, but it sounded more like a mockingbird's rasp than Ma's sweet sounds of joy.

'You're beautiful, Hester.' Ma came up behind her in a gentle breeze of lavender and delicate rose perfume. They were fragrances that had defined Ma for as long as Hester could remember. Ma pressed her cheek against Hester's. 'My precious daughter,' she said.

Hester held the mirror further away until it captured both of their faces in the glass. The warm yellow light of the candle flame made their images turn golden. But the image of Hester behind the glass showed no similarities to Ma, so Hester studied her reflection again, seeking a resemblance to Pa. As her search grew more desperate, Francis Billington's look of pity crept into her thoughts.

Ma took the mirror from Hester's hand. 'Something is troubling you, Hester. Tell me what it is so I may put your mind at ease.'

'It's nothing, Ma.' Hester grasped the edge of the casket as the room seemed to tilt and spin. A dreadful thought had seeded itself, and the more she tried to dismiss it, the more the thought took hold. With such a lack of family resemblance, was she someone else's child?

CHAPTER 5

'HESTER, are you sickening for something? You've been out of sorts for days.' Ma entered the bedchamber and bustled towards her, the wooden soles and heels of her shoes clacking across the floorboards. 'You've spent so long alone up here this evening, we all thought you'd retired for the night.' She tipped Hester's face up towards her and pressed her fingers to her forehead and the back of her neck. 'You don't have a fever. There's no bloom in your cheeks.'

Hester lowered her mother's hand. 'I am well, Ma. A little tired, perhaps. It has been a long and busy day.' She had spent the morning making house calls with Ma, examining and reassuring four mothers-to-be. Then she had spent the afternoon in the still room making unguents and lavender-scented soap. After spending so many hours on her feet, her joints throbbed and her calf muscles ached. Hester loosened the laces of her left boot and eased out her foot. Then she peeled off her stocking and massaged the burning skin over her misshapen joints.

Ma picked up the boot and frowned. 'I'm sorry I refused your request for a new pair, Hester. I can see where the leather has worn thin, and it looks like one of the metal rods might have snapped.'

Hester gingerly touched the sore that had not healed since Elizabeth Alden's wedding.

Ma grimaced. 'I didn't realise you were suffering so.'

'Yes, well, Martha must have her new shoes first. It wouldn't do for her to go about the town in cumbersome clogs.' Hester bristled at her own petulance. 'Forgive me, Ma. I did not mean to sound churlish.'

Ma placed the boot on the floorboards and rose to her feet. 'No, Hester, you were not being churlish. Martha can wait a while longer for shoes, but your boots need replacing now. We will visit the cordwainer tomorrow morning.'

Hester enjoyed the small swell of triumph that bubbled up in her chest. At last, her needs had taken priority over Martha's. But the triumph soon shattered as a wave of guilt swept through her. Pride was not a trait she wished to share with her sister. She preferred to be known for kindness and generosity – she preferred to be like her mother. Ma must be her mother! Neither Ma nor Pa had ever said a word to suggest that Hester was not theirs. She felt Ma's gaze boring into her as if sensing her inner turmoil.

'I can wait for new boots, Ma. I'm sure Pa can replace the broken rod.'

Ma shook her head. 'I have made my decision, Hester.' She turned and left the bedchamber with a swoosh of her skirts. She returned a few moments later with the small mirror in her hand and held it out to Hester.

'I'd like you to have this.'

'But Ma, that mirror is special to you!'

'That's the very reason I would like you to have it.' Ma pressed the handle of the mirror into Hester's hand, folding her fingers around the metal that had worn smooth and thin from many years of handling. 'This helped me to feel connected to my mother even though there was an ocean between us.' Ma looked deep into Hester's eyes. 'I have treasured it for many years. It's your turn to treasure it now. May it help you feel connected to me when the day comes for us to part.'

Hester tightened her grasp on the tarnished metal. It seemed heavier than usual and cool in her hand. Her throat constricted as she murmured her gratitude for a gift that felt bittersweet. She waited for her mother to retreat from the room and patter down the stairs, then threw the mirror onto her bed so it landed with the glass face down. As much as Hester had always loved the trinket with its elegant swirling frame, she vowed to store it in a chest and never look at it again.

CHAPTER 6

THE CORDWAINER ASSURED Hester that her new boots would be ready by the end of the week. With her mood lifted by the thought of new footwear, Hester excused herself from the cordwainer's house and left her mother talking to his wife. Climbing the hill that led to the grist mill, Hester went in search of a tree she had heard was still heavy with walnuts despite the rapid approach of November. A biting breeze whipped around her legs, flapping her skirts and tilting her hat. She pressed her hat back into place with one hand and tightened her grasp of her walking stick with the other. It was only a matter of weeks before the first snowfall would arrive with the icy grip of another winter.

Hester intended to make an apple tart topped with crumbled walnuts. It was her mother's favourite pie, and Hester thought it would make the perfect gift to thank her for the new boots. Instead of drying the nuts in the loft for a few weeks, she would toast them with a little honey before smashing them into a powder and sprinkling them over the fruit. She located the tree and shook the lowest branches, yielding a flurry of ripe walnuts. She knelt on the soft moss-covered ground and started filling a cloth bag with a bounty of green husks.

A rustling of leaves made Hester pause. She heard a soft nicker of a horse and a delicate snort as it picked its way over tree roots. She used her stick to push herself up and turned to see Adam leading the horse towards her. Hester felt her cheeks glow pink.

'Master Phillips! I mean, Adam. Good day to you.'

'It is indeed a good day, Hester.' He nodded towards the bulging cloth bag she was holding. 'The fruit and nut harvest has been generous this year.'

'It has.' She swallowed. 'What brings you this way today?'

Adam stroked the horse's neck. 'We're on our way to the governor's house. This poor fellow had a sharp stone lodged deep in his hoof that was causing him to limp. I've cleaned out all of his hooves and fitted him with new iron shoes. I thought I'd walk him for a while to check that all is well, and I'm happy to report that his limp is now cured.'

Hester shuffled her feet, acutely aware of her mud-smeared boots. She wished someone could cure her limp with such a simple solution.

Adam took the bag of walnuts out of Hester's hands and slung the bag's handles over one shoulder. 'It would be my pleasure to walk with you if you are heading home.'

'I'd like that, Adam,' Hester said, the words catching in her throat.

They proceeded down the hill at a gentle pace until the

horse stopped beside a verge to nibble some grass. When it stopped the second time, Adam's hand brushed against Hester's. His touch was light but it made Hester's blood run hot and caused her skin to tingle. She turned her head to look at him and caught a movement under his jerkin.

'What was that?' Hester asked, taking a step away from him.

Adam's lips broadened into a smile. 'Ah, my little friend wishes to make your acquaintance.'

'Your friend?'

'I named him Shadow because that describes him well.' Adam lowered the bag of walnuts to the ground. 'Wherever I go, he comes with me.' He reached into his jerkin and lifted out a small bundle of fur. Hester took a sharp intake of breath. The ball of fur was a squirrel, and Ma said squirrels were vermin.

Adam settled Shadow on his large palm. The squirrel lifted its tail and spread it over its back.

Hester wrinkled her nose with disgust. 'Why hide that creature under your clothes?'

Adam stroked the squirrel's head with his forefinger. 'I don't hide him. Not really. He uses my jerkin as a nest. He's a dear little creature but unable to fend for himself.'

'Why?'

Adam lifted the squirrel from his palm and pointed to its hind legs. Half of one leg was missing. 'He must have escaped from a trap or a fox but left part of his leg behind. I treated the stump with a poultice. I'm lucky he's still alive.'

'You mean *he's* lucky he's still alive. My mother would have killed him and put him in a stew.' Hester was softening towards the stricken creature, whose eyes were as shiny as polished jet beads.

'I'm pleased to have earned his trust. He's an entertaining little fellow.'

'Does your mother allow you to keep him in the house?'

Adam chuckled. 'She's used to my habit of rescuing strays.' He pointed to the bag of walnuts. 'May I give him one of those? Walnuts are his favourite.'

Hester nodded and retrieved one herself. She squeezed the split husk to pop out the inner hard shell. It fell from her hand and struck the ground with a muted thud. She broke the shell with the heel of her boot and picked up one of the broken pieces, placing it in the middle of her palm and offering it to the squirrel. Shadow flicked his head up and down as if excited by the gift, then snatched up the bounty with his tiny paws and nibbled at the nut meat.

'Now he's your friend, too.' Adam helped the squirrel climb back inside his jerkin and then retrieved Hester's bag of walnuts. 'My mother calls me a rescuer of lost souls, but I don't see it that way. We all have a purpose in life. I like to think that mine is rescuing injured animals. I could leave them to die and provide food for hungry predators, but I wouldn't do that to an injured child, so why would I do that to an animal?'

'That explains why you're kindly towards me. I'm like one of your animals needing your pity.'

Adam appeared dismayed at Hester's comment. 'No, Hester, I do not pity you. I respect you. Your father might be our town's physician and your mother might deliver many babes, but both of your parents, as kind as they are, can be snappy with those whom they treat. In situations demanding empathy and a gentle manner, it's you people seek. My grandmother is especially fond of you. She refuses to allow anyone but you to steep herbs for her ailments and make unguents for her skin.' He looked sideways at Hester. 'You have something that sets you apart from everyone else – and I'm not referring to whatever ails your foot and your leg.'

Hester took a moment or two to reflect on Adam's words. There had been several occasions when her mother had spoken with a sharper tongue than necessary, and many a time, Ma spoiled food when she was cooking because of her impatience. Her father often slid into a temper if he could not determine a difficult diagnosis and grew agitated with his patients if they questioned a treatment he prescribed. Hester approached every task with calm deliberation, be that cleaning, stitching, baking, gardening or brewing. She had never snapped at a labouring mother nor rolled her eyes. She was the calmest member of her family and the one her siblings turned to in a crisis.

Adam's compliments gave Hester comfort as they resumed their walk in silence. But then his words weighed heavily as she drew closer to her home. Now there was no denying how she differed from the rest of her family. She did not share even a single similarity in her nature or her appearance.

CHAPTER 7

HESTER LEFT Ma to settle the bill and stepped outside the cordwainer's workshop. Her new boots glowed like chestnuts in the November sunlight, and the cordwainer had softened the leather between the concealed rods to reduce the pressure against bony prominences. Hester walked along the road and turned onto another street but quickly withdrew to one side as a young herdsman approached leading a pair of Red Devon cattle. Hester looked from the cattle to her boots. They were almost identical in colour. A screech from a bird of prey drew her attention skyward. Its dark silhouette circled high above her, its form too small to make an accurate identification. A falcon perhaps, or possibly a hawk. After the cattle had passed her by, Hester stepped out onto the rutted road and watched the bird soar through the air in wide sweeping arcs. She strained to make out the shape of its wings and tail, but the bird broke from its circling, flew northward and disappeared.

Something struck the back of Hester's left knee,

causing her leg to buckle. She shifted her weight onto her stick but not fast enough to stop herself from crumpling to the ground. A loud splintering crack rang out from the middle of her walking stick as the wood fractured and snapped in two. Hester fought back tears as she gathered her senses and prepared to rise to her feet. As she put her weight through her left hand, her palm pressed into something soft and damp. She glanced at the object and recoiled in horror. It was a ball made out of a pig's bladder. The bladder had ripped, oozing its contents, and her fingers had become smeared with wet earth mixed with mushy rotten peelings and foul-smelling dung. Hester turned to look over her shoulder. Two gangly youths were watching her and sniggering, their cruel, spotty faces flushed with mirth. The shorter of the youths pointed at her and then mimicked the way she walked.

'Why don't you get off your backside and show him how to do it right?' shouted the taller one. 'I'm certain your waddle has a roll more akin to this.' He staggered towards her, listing to one side then the other. He walked like a man who had spent a long night in a tavern and almost lost the use of his legs.

Hester bit back a retort. She crawled towards the opposite side of the road, making her way towards a bench nestled by the front wall of a house. She pulled herself up and sat on it, taking care not to brush her soiled hand against her wool skirt. The boys raced to the pig's bladder and kicked it back and forth, each strike of a foot causing it to bleed more of its filth. Hester tried to ignore them, bracing herself for her walk home, but the smell of animal dung wafted from her hand as a pungent reminder of their cruelty.

'Look out!' the tallest youth shouted before kicking the broken ball towards Hester.

Hester jerked her legs to one side to avoid a second impact. Both youths approached and loomed over her. She shrank away from them until her back pressed against the clapboard wall of the house.

'Looks like a pig and smells like a pig. She's even covered in shit!'

Both youths bellowed with laughter.

'Leave me alone!' Hester tried to swallow a sob.

The shorter boy leered at Hester and then pinched his nostrils closed. 'No one wants a pig for a daughter. Not even her own parents.'

The air seemed to cool around Hester. She shuddered. 'What did you say?'

'Move away, you ignorant little delinquents! Leave this young woman alone.'

Hester's cheeks burned with shame as she watched Adam stride towards them. He had a large leather bag draped across his body, and it rattled with every step. Adam dropped the bag to the ground with a loud clank of metal against metal.

The younger boy elbowed the taller youth's side. 'Me thinks the young blacksmith has fallen in love.'

'Away with you both. Go!'

The oldest boy wrinkled his nose with distaste. 'He could do better than her,' he said, leading the other boy away.

'Don't forget this,' Adam yelled after them.

As the boys turned, Adam kicked the diminished bladder with the toe of his boot. Hester stifled a smile as it struck the side of the taller youth's thigh and slid down his breeches and stocking, leaving a putrid dark trail.

'New to the town,' Adam said, shaking his head. 'Such disgraceful behaviour for the sons of strict Puritans. They won't bother you again.' Adam retrieved the pieces of Hester's walking stick and added them to his bag before proffering his arm. Hester accepted his offer of help to stand and took care not to touch him with her stinking, soiled hand.

'Hold tight, Hester. I will walk you home.'

Tears of humiliation spilled onto Hester's cheeks. 'Please forgive my weeping,' she said. 'The filth is easy enough to clean, but I shall be housebound without my walking stick.'

Adam gave her arm a reassuring squeeze. 'Not for long, dear Hester. With your permission, I will take the pieces home with me and carve a new walking stick to match the length. It might not be as elegant as this one, but I promise it will be strong. My uncle is a gifted wood-carver, and he's teaching me his skills. I'll start carving a new stick this evening and use every spare minute to work on it. I'll deliver it to your house soon after I finish it.'

Hester felt a rush of affection. 'Thank you, Adam. You are the kindest of friends.'

They made slow progress along the dirt road in companionable silence. A sharp breeze blew in from the ocean, carrying the cool scent of sea spray and a warning of bitter weather to come. Hester shivered.

Something one boy had said niggled her. 'Why did he say that?'

'Say what?'

'One of those youths said my parents did not want me. I have my imperfections, but Ma has never uttered a cruel word nor made me feel unwanted.'

'Ah.'

Hester heard Adam catch a breath. Her chest tightened. She pulled hard on Adam's arm, leaving him no choice but to stop walking and face her. 'What did he mean? I sense you and he both know something I do not.'

Adam clenched his lower lip between his teeth.

'Adam, if you too have heard a rumour or overheard something my mother said about me, I insist you tell me now. We are friends, are we not?'

'Yes, but—'

'Friends do not hide things from one another.'

Adam shook his head. 'I can't.'

'Please.'

Adam furrowed his brow. After a long moment of contemplation, he turned his gaze back to Hester. 'Very well. I think he was referring to something that occurred a week or two ago. I overheard part of a conversation, and he was a party to it.'

'What conversation?' Hester's heart thundered beneath her ribs.

'Your father spoke with his mother after the morning Sabbath service. They were discussing the perils of childbirth and how often young mothers die.'

'What does that have to do with me?'

Adam opened his mouth as if he was going to speak again but then thought better of it.

'Well?' Hester persisted. Her voice sounded shrill.

Adam lowered his leather bag to the rutted surface of the road. He took Hester's hand in his and stroked the back of her fingers with the pad of his thumb.

Hester stared at her skin as if expecting a trail of fire left by his touch. 'There's clearly more you have to say, Adam. Whatever it is, I insist you tell me now.'

Adam tightened his grip on her fingers. 'It pains me to say this, Hester, but...' His voice trailed away.

'For goodness' sake, are you going to tell me or not?'

Adam took a slow breath and looked deep into her eyes. A trail of emotions flickered across his face. Sadness. Regret. Sympathy. 'I didn't catch every word he said, but he mentioned problems with your birth and said—'

Hester wrenched her hand free, cutting Adam short. 'So, my mother had a difficult time giving birth to me! Were you going to say she died, for clearly she did not!' Her voice became sharper. 'And if my parents had rejected me, they would not have brought me to live here.'

Adam let out a sigh. 'It was wrong of me to mention that conversation. I probably misheard what was said. Forgive me for speaking out of turn.'

Hester did not reply and turned away from Adam. How she wished she could use her stick and continue home without him. She heard the clanking of Adam's tools as he retrieved his bag. Soon he was beside her again and linked his arm through hers. They continued their walk in silence. As their footsteps crunched across stony ground, Hester did not dare turn her head. She feared that if she met Adam's gaze, she would unleash a flood of tears. She found it perplexing that he sided with the youths rather than dismissing every word they had said. Her parents would never reject a child with any kind of flaw, be that a crooked spine or a twisted foot – and they never expressed revulsion if a child was born deformed. Ma might have had a hard labour, but she had never discussed it at home. If she had struggled during her travail, by God's grace she had survived and borne another daughter and a son.

As Hester's home came into view, Ma opened the door. Hester watched her bid farewell to a visitor before noticing Hester and Adam approach. Ma's lips broke into a smile as she waved to them both.

Hester nudged Adam hard with her elbow. 'That was a mean thing you tried to imply, Adam. There is my mother, delighted to see me, and very much alive and well.'

CHAPTER 8

'My dear, you are an angel, just like your mother.'

Hester smiled at the elderly woman who had come to have her leg ulcer dressed. After cleaning out a pungent discharge, Hester had smothered the ulcer with a fragrant ointment made with chamomile and rose. 'It's kind of you to say so, Widow Morton,' she said, tying a linen bandage around the widow's lower leg. 'I try to be gentle, but sometimes it's impossible to avoid causing pain.'

Widow Morton curled her gnarled fingers around Hester's wrist. 'Alas, that is the case in so many things.' She tightened her grip. 'You have a kindness about you, Hester. Be sure never to lose it.' She released Hester's wrist and withdrew a small but bulging linen pouch from inside her jacket. 'This should be enough money to cover my last few visits.' She pressed the pouch into Hester's hand.

Hester caught a whiff of musty fabric as she accepted the pouch. She took a quick peek inside. 'This is too much,' she said, spying a shilling nestled among the coins.

Widow Morton dismissed her protest with a wave. 'If I have truly overpaid, you may keep the surplus for yourself. I imagine it won't be too long before you're setting up a home of your own. You will need coins when that day comes.'

'Thank you,' Hester said, tightening her fingers around the pouch. 'But I doubt I'll ever have a home of my own.'

'None of us can predict the future, my dear, but all of us can hope. I'll see myself out.'

Hester watched Widow Morton hobble across the room. She gave Hester a fond smile before stepping outdoors and closing the front door behind her with a gentle click of the latch. Ma joined Hester at the table with a waft of lavender and sea-herb soap. 'She's a dear old soul, isn't she? And you know, Hester, she will only permit *you* to treat her ulcers now.'

'She said I'm like you, Ma. She said that we are angels.' Hester shook the linen pouch and held it out to her mother.

'That pouch is yours, Hester.' Ma gently pushed Hester's hand away. 'She was very clear about that.'

Hester tipped a few coins onto her palm. They were scratched and dented and cool against her skin. 'Am I really like you?'

Hester thought she heard her mother catch a breath, but Ma's face shone with joy as she tipped Hester's face to look at her. 'You show great promise as a young midwife, and we both love to immerse ourselves in the study of books. We both make excellent nurses and can treat all manner of ills. So yes, Hester, we are very much alike.'

'But I don't share any of your mannerisms or funny

little habits. Martha twirls her hair like you when she reads a book, and Samuel has Pa's frown and his brooding pout.'

'But we both have a skill for drawing.' Ma plucked a journal from a pile of books on the table. She opened it to a random page. 'Look how well you've drawn these flowers. See how your style is very close to mine.'

'But I don't look like you.'

Ma shook her head. A strange expression skittered across her face, and her hands seemed to tremble for a moment. 'No, you do not, but I am glad of it. You have a beautiful face and eyes that sparkle like jewels. I wouldn't want your face to resemble mine. Yours is perfect as it is.'

'I'm far from perfect.' Hester clenched her teeth, fearing she might cry.

'We all have flaws, Hester. But it's not our flaws that define us, it's the things we do, the way we treat other people and how we live our lives.' She paused for a moment, furrowing her brow. 'Think about it, Hester.' The lines in Ma's brow faded, and she gave Hester a loving smile. 'Not all children resemble their parents. You only have to think about our neighbours to see that for yourself. Their youngest boy has flame-red hair, while the rest of the family have brown. We both know he's Mary's child because we delivered him ourselves.'

Hester had to acknowledge that Ma was right. The little boy bore no resemblance to either parent or his siblings. She chastised herself for worrying about something so petty and determined to make more effort to dismiss any further doubts.

CHAPTER 9

Nᴏᴠᴇᴍʙᴇʀ ɢᴀᴠᴇ ᴡᴀʏ ᴛᴏ Dᴇᴄᴇᴍʙᴇʀ. The air turned frigid and the rain turned into snow, leaving clumps of snowflakes clinging to the windowsills and creeping up the mottled glass.

'Slide the shutter across, Hester, and close the drapes. There's a chill creeping into the room.'

'Yes, Ma.' Hester tried to hide her exasperation. Several weeks had passed since her walking stick snapped. Unable to venture outside the house, she missed the sights and sounds of the harbour. Few ships visited the colony during the long winter months, but the fishing fleet still sailed most days, and she longed to see the skiffs dancing across the water with their sails billowing in the breeze.

A blazing fire was burning in the hearth, crackling and popping and giving off a pleasant smell of woodsmoke. Hester was leaning against the wall by the window using the cooler air near the glass to draw heat from her cheeks while she watched passers-by trudge through the snow. As she went to move the shutter, she spied a familiar figure hurrying along the street. She dragged the shutter across the glass, closing it with a thud, then shuffled sideways for a few steps and opened the front door.

'Hester! What are you—?'

Hester cut her mother off mid-sentence. 'It's Adam.'

'Adam who?' Ma rose from her chair and smoothed the creases from her skirts. She pulled a ribbon from her hair and shook it loose before gathering it in one hand and tying it up again. Hester smiled. Her mother was always so careful to maintain a respectable appearance, but no matter how hard she tried, there was always a lock of hair that dangled out of place.

'Adam Phillips. The blacksmith's son.' Hester turned back towards the white world outdoors. Her smile broadened. Adam was carrying a walking stick. 'Pray, come in,' Hester said, ushering him inside. She closed the door behind him and watched powdery snow drop from his cloak as he stamped his boots on the coarse rush mat.

'Good morrow, Master Trelawney, Mistress Trelawney.' Adam removed a wide-brimmed hat and held it to his chest. He gave a small bow to Martha and nodded a greeting to Samuel. He turned towards Hester and held out an elegant walking stick. 'Here it is, as promised. Forgive me, it took longer than expected, but I hope it's to your liking.'

Hester accepted the stick and ran her fingertips over the handle. It felt warm to the touch despite having travelled to her through the ice-cold air outdoors. 'Did you make this by yourself?'

Adam's cheeks flushed. 'Almost. My uncle showed me how to carve the spirals without weakening the wood, but apart from that quick demonstration, it's all my own work.'

Hester traced the neat spiral grooves at the lower end of the stick's shaft. They developed into a creeping twist of ivy interwoven with delicate wild roses. The handle was smooth and was shaped so that it fit into her hand.

'It's beautiful.'

Pa crossed the room and took the walking stick from Hester. 'You have produced a fine piece of carving here,' he said to Adam. 'Far better than anything I could have done.'

Hester watched Adam's flush deepen and spread to his neck and his jaw. 'Thank you, sir. I appreciate the praise. The gentlemen of Boston have taken to using walking sticks as apparel. My uncle sells the sticks he makes and has offered to sell any I make too. He knows I'm eager to save money to start a business of my own.'

'That's going to take a lot of walking sticks,' Pa said, patting Adam on the back of his upper arm.

'Yes, sir, it will, but I'm a hard worker. I'll toil for my father by day and I'll make walking sticks in the evenings. I hope to have my own farriery workshop one day.' He turned his head a little to one side and met Hester's admiring gaze. 'I'd like to build a barn too, where I can care for sick and injured animals.'

Pa gave an approving grunt. 'God willing, it all works out for you.'

A jangling sound drew their attention as Ma lifted a pot from a shelf and reached inside for coins. 'Let me pay you for Hester's new walking stick.'

Adam raised his hand in protest. 'No, Mistress

Trelawney. This walking stick is my gift to Hester.' He lowered his head as if embarrassed. 'There's another reason I came to your door today on such an inclement afternoon. My sister is in labour. She wasn't in any distress when I left home, but my mother asked if you would attend to her.'

Hester's mother smiled. 'It will be our pleasure, won't it, Hester?'

Hester felt a lightness in her chest. She had missed several births while she had been confined to the house. How she missed watching young mothers hold their babies for the first time! She had had to settle for discussing the deliveries with Ma and describing how she would have handled any complications. If she could prove to Ma that she knew what to do, Ma might let her attend birthing mothers by herself. The sooner she was a visible presence in the town, the better for establishing her own reputation. *Hester Trelawney, the town's young midwife*. It sounded so good in her mind.

Martha rose from her chair and scurried from the room. She returned with Ma's delivery bag and Ma's and Hester's fur-lined cloaks. She helped Ma into her cloak and then did the same for Hester. As she draped the cloak across Hester's shoulders, she leaned so close that her breath tickled Hester's ear. 'Me thinks love is in the air,' she whispered, squeezing Hester's shoulders.

'Don't be ridiculous,' Hester murmured. She stroked the petals of one of the roses carved into her walking stick. 'We are simply the best of friends.'

CHAPTER 10

I<small>T WAS</small> bitter in the yard behind the Phillips' house. The chill crept through Hester's bones and caused her chest to tighten. She picked her way across the snow-covered ground, walking stick in one hand and a tied bundle of soiled linens in the other. She dropped the linens onto the fire that Master Phillips had prepared and coaxed to a roaring blaze. *Far better to dispose of the sheets out here*, Hester thought, as thick, grey, pungent smoke curled up from the flames and prickled the insides of her nostrils and mouth.

A full moon hung low in the night sky, casting a pearlescent glow over the blacksmith's snow-coated house and outbuildings. A horse peered out from a stall, its breath rising in white puffy clouds. Hester took careful steps towards the stables and reached up to stroke the horse's cheek. The horse made a soft snorting sound and then withdrew to the shadows of its stall, leaving a trail of breath sweetened by the smell of hay. Hester adored horses. She hoped that one day she might ride one and gallop along the shoreline, tasting the salty sea breeze while the wind blew through her hair. A sharp pain deep in the bones of her left foot caused her to dismiss the thought as quickly as it came. Her dream was nothing but a foolish fantasy.

Hester returned to the house and paused beside a table to study a sketch. She touched a picture of a young rabbit sniffing a holly bush, the image so detailed that Hester fancied she could stroke its silky fur.

'That's one of Adam's,' his mother said. She handed Hester a pouch containing coins as payment for her and Ma's attendance. Hester always felt awkward accepting payment for attending a woman's birth but supposed she would have to get used to it if she was to earn her living as a midwife.

Mistress Phillips moved the rabbit sketch aside to reveal another magnificent drawing, this time of a mare with her foal. 'This is Adam's latest. He finished it two days ago.'

'Your horses?' Hester asked.

Adam's mother shook her head. 'Drawn from an image in his mind.'

Hester examined the details of the picture. She could see every hair of the mare's mane and almost feel the power in her leg muscles. The new mother had a look of concern as she watched her foal trotting along beside her.

'He's a talented artist.'

Mistress Phillips nodded. 'Yes, he is. When he sets his mind to something, he perseveres until it is precisely the way he wants it.'

Hester imagined Adam sitting at the table with a thin

piece of charcoal in his hand, moving it across the paper to create the animals he loved. There was a gentle side to Adam, unusual for young men of his age. One day he would make a kind husband for a fortunate bride. Hester checked herself and cleared her mind. She had work to do.

When Hester re-entered the bedchamber, she found her mother perched on the edge of the bed, instructing Adam's sister on how to breastfeed her newborn daughter.

'It's time we went home,' Hester said, watching the baby suckle and admiring the shock of copper-coloured hair that was a perfect match with the mother's.

Ma rose to her feet and swept the back of her hand across her brow. 'I'll be glad of some sleep,' she said, giving Hester a warm smile. 'I didn't expect to be here until almost dawn.'

They arrived home before sunrise, but Pa was already up and about and he had set a fire in the hearth. He took one look at Ma's wan face and insisted she retire to bed.

'After I've written up the notes about the birth,' Ma said, reaching up with both hands towards the delivery ledger, intending to take it from its special place on one of the bookshelves.

'Can Hester do that for you?'

Ma dropped her arms to her sides, clearly growing a little exasperated. 'I like to write up the notes, Jed.'

'Does Hester know all the details?'

'I do,' Hester said. 'I delivered the child, and there were no complications.'

Pa nodded. 'Then Hester should write the notes.'

Ma had never permitted Hester to add entries to the ledger. Hester looked at her mother with entreating eyes. 'Ma? I'm not ready to sleep yet. You allowed me to deliver the baby so permit me to write in the ledger too.'

Ma seemed to wrestle with the idea but then covered her mouth and yawned. 'Please, Hester. If you would. Exhaustion overwhelms me.'

Hester removed her cloak and settled at the table. Pa took the ledger from the shelf and put it on the table in front of her, then fetched a wax candle that was burning with a tall bright flame. Hester pulled the candle towards her until it cast a disc of golden orange light across the ledger. The leather cover of the ledger was as soft as velvet and enclosed a thick bundle of pages, most of them already filled with Ma's neat handwriting. Hester turned to a clean page. She wrote Adam's sister's name at the top, and then, in her neatest script, she added the date of the baby's birth. She recorded the normal shape of her back and that she had all of her fingers and toes. Next, Hester recorded that the placenta had come away in one piece and that blood loss had not been excessive. She made a note about the soothing rose oil she had used and the chamomile tisane and how long it had taken after delivery for the baby to learn to suckle. Hester turned to the previous entry to check she had missed no details. Satisfied she had omitted nothing, she blew across the paper to encourage the ink to dry. She closed the ledger and stroked the leather of its timeworn cover. It held the details of hundreds of deliveries – an accurate historical record maintained by her mother. Hester moved the candle closer, eager to read the details of Ma's earliest deliveries. She opened the ledger to the first page and read the earliest entry. The date was 1623, and Leyden was the location. There was the name of the mother followed by the words "Safe delivery of baby boy. No complications or deformities". Hester scanned the next few entries, imagining her mother at each delivery, revelling in every miracle of new life she had brought into the world. From 1625, Ma's notes were more detailed. She included the day, month and year of birth, the street name, town and duration of labour. Most entries included the name of the child. A few of them did not. 'Those parents took longer to name their children,' Hester murmured. 'Ma would not have known what names those parents chose.' Hester flicked forward to the entries for 1626, the year of her own birth. She read the details about dainty twin girls and a lusty boy named Ichabod. She stalled at an entry at the bottom of a page, unsettled by its lack of information. The year was 1626, but the day and month were absent. Hester caught her breath as she read the scanty details:

Mother's name: Hester Twisselton

Child: Baby Girl

Under the heading "Complications", the entry had been left blank.

Hester is not a common name, she thought, flicking through more pages. *I wonder if my birth record is in here.* But Hester soon dismissed that thought, for Ma wouldn't have recorded the details of her own labour. She found a record of another mother named Hester who had given birth to a baby boy, perfectly formed and with no complications during delivery. Hester turned back to the entry for Hester Twisselton. It was the only one that lacked detail from 1625 onwards. Ma would not have forgotten what happened, so why the lack of information? Hester considered asking her mother but then thought of a plausible reason. *Perhaps the mother died.* The taunting youths crept into her mind, as well as Adam's description of an overheard conversation. The words on the page wobbled and shifted until Hester could not read them at all. She pushed the ledger away as a headache gripped her like a vice. The only conclusion she could draw cut through her heart like a knife.

CHAPTER 11

HESTER ROSE before Ma and spent the afternoon sweeping the floor in the meeting room of the fort and adding a layer of beeswax to the tables and benches. The hours had dragged, and Hester was eager to return home and confront her mother about the incomplete entry in the ledger. She heard her parents' voices long before she reached the front door. Never had she heard them argue like this. She quickened her pace, concerned something dreadful had happened, but stopped before she drew level with the window. Ma was screeching at Pa. Pa's voice was loud but calm as he tried to pacify Ma. Hester thought better of interrupting, preferring to give them a couple of minutes to allow the situation to cool before entering the house. She lowered her basket to the ground and leaned against the wall. Her back was sore from bending forward for long periods of time. Ma continued to rail at Pa and then uttered words that sent a chill through Hester.

'She will never forgive us for this!'

Hester's heart rose into her throat. The snow-filled sky

seemed to press down on her. 'Desire, listen to me!' Her father's voice had grown more urgent. 'That girl knows we have always done our best for her, and we will continue to do so. But the time has come! Tell me you agree.'

Pa lowered his voice, and Hester did not catch his next words. Her thoughts were reeling. Time for what? Were they going to send her away? Her lips quivered. Two of her closest friends had left for Boston, sent away by their parents the previous month to serve in prominent households. Was she about to share their fate? She had no wish to leave Plimoth! And why had Pa referred to her as "that girl"? She moved towards the door and pressed her gloved hands against the wood, steeling herself to go inside. Her breath turned fast and shallow as a wave of dread washed over her, and the ledger entry about Hester Twisselton started to taunt her. Hester clenched her fingers and tried to steady her breathing. Her parents were still arguing, although Ma was no longer shouting. Hester could not bring herself to lift the latch and open the door. She moved back towards the window. Although it was closed, she could hear every word that passed between Ma and Pa.

'She knows, Jed.'

'How can she? We've not uttered a word about it in her presence, and we have confided in very few people here.'

'Because of this.'

Hester squinted through the window, struggling to see into the gloom beyond the mottled glass. Her mother was pointing at something on the table. The delivery ledger. It was still open from when she had been studying its pages much earlier that morning.

'We agreed we wouldn't keep it from her.' There was a muffled thud as Pa slammed the ledger shut. 'I wanted to tell her when she was young so that she grew up with the idea instead of it coming as a shock. But you insisted upon waiting, and still you refrain from telling her!'

'I did not want her to know.'

Hester had heard enough. She snatched up her basket and flung the door open, slamming it hard against the wall. She hurled her basket towards a corner, spilling her cleaning rags onto the floorboards.

'Hester!' Ma paled and exchanged a nervous glance with Pa.

'What is it you did not want me to know?' Hester removed her cape and peeled off her gloves. She fixed Ma with a hard stare.

Pa cleared his throat. 'Hester, will you sit for a moment?' He gestured towards the table.

Hester shook her head and leaned heavily on her stick to take the weight off her left foot.

'Hester, dearest…' Ma began to weep. 'I believe you may have stumbled across a secret. Something we should have told you long ago.'

Hester's limbs shook. She felt cold and light-headed. 'Well?' Her voice was little more than a croak. 'Tell me now!'

'Please, Hester. Let us all sit for this conversation.' Pa reached out to take Hester by the arm, but Hester pushed his hand away. The room seemed to tilt and turn. Hester grasped the table edge. Pa was right. It would be better to sit. She staggered across the room to the chair nearest the hearth. When her parents joined her, she glared from one to the other. Neither Ma nor Pa uttered a word.

It was Hester who broke the silence. 'Tell me who I am.'

Pa fidgeted in his chair and tugged at a loose thread on his breeches. 'You are Hester Trelawney,' he said, 'and have been since the day you were born.'

'Are you certain of that, Pa?' Hester's voice sounded odd, as if she were listening to another person speaking in the distance. Her heart raced. 'I think I might be Hester Twisselton, going by what I read – or rather didn't read – in Ma's delivery ledger.' Hester glared at Ma. 'I'm right, aren't I? My mother's name was Hester Twisselton. I'm not a Trelawney at all.' Ma lowered her gaze and stared at her fingers. Her hands were trembling. Hester pressed on with more questions. 'Why is the entry incomplete? And why did you keep the truth from me?'

Ma pressed her lips together. Eventually she blurted out, 'You are our daughter in all but blood.'

A sob caught in Hester's throat. 'But it's my blood that would have connected us!' She slapped the armrest of her chair. 'I demand to know what happened to my mother! My real mother!'

Pa leaned forward in his chair and reached for Hester's hand. 'Hester—'

'Don't!' Hester pressed her hands to her face, covering her eyes as she sobbed. Tears fell, soaking her cheeks, and Hester had to fight to compose herself. She glared at the woman who had pretended to be her mother for almost eighteen years. 'Well? Are you going to tell me about my mother or not?'

Hester watched Ma grasp a fold of skirt in each hand and clench it between her fingers. She gripped the fabric so hard that her knuckles paled. Tears spilled onto her cheeks. 'She died, Hester. The Good Lord saw fit to take her moments after you were born.'

Hester gasped. She had already presumed as much from the lack of detail in the ledger, but to hear it spoken aloud made it feel too real. Her heart ached for the mother she would never know. 'And my father? What happened to him?'

'We don't know.' Ma's voice cracked. 'He said he could not raise you after your mother passed. I tried to persuade him, but your father fled. That's why we took you in.'

Pa rose from his chair and knelt before Hester. 'Please know that we love you, Hester, and we cherish you as much as Samuel and Martha.'

A rustle of skirts drew Hester's attention towards the corner of the room, where Martha stood with her hands pressed to her cheeks and her mouth rounded into an 'o'. So, her sister had not known the truth either. A new hurt caused Hester's heart to ache. They weren't sisters at all.

The months of doubt and the feelings of not belonging crashed over Hester and drowned her in a deep well of sorrow. She rose from the chair and made slow progress climbing the stairs, needing to be alone in her bedchamber. Every step seemed to grow steeper and her limbs became heavier and harder to move. She was no longer the physician's eldest daughter. She was the daughter of a dead woman and a father who had disappeared. Hester lay on her bed and stared up at the ceiling, her misery blurring her vision. Weetamoo's words came back to haunt her. "The Chosen One", she had called her. Weetamoo had known the truth all along. 'Dear God,' Hester murmured. 'Help me make sense of this.' She dried her eyes with the backs of her hands. 'Help me understand who I am. Who is Hester Twisselton?'

CHAPTER 12

HESTER WOKE early after a restless night. She turned onto her back and gazed up at the ceiling where a few cobwebs shimmered on a joist, illuminated by a narrow shard of moonlight that cut through a chink in the window drapes. Cold floorboards popped beyond the bedchamber door. An owl hooted from somewhere in the distance, defending its territory or calling to its mate. Martha continued sleeping peacefully, her breathing slow and deep. Hester eased herself out of the bed, taking care not to disturb her.

The night air was brisk against Hester's skin, and she had to use her knuckles to break the thin layer of ice that had formed in her washbowl. After a quick rinse of her hands and face, she pulled on her clothes: a clean shift, her favourite wool skirt and a matching russet jacket. She put her boots on the floor side by side and tied their laces together to make them easier to carry, then draped the knotted-together laces around her neck so that the two boots rested on her chest. She made her way towards the stairs and clutched the handrail with both hands, fearing her ankle might give way as she silently placed her stockinged feet on each narrow step. She perched on the bottom stair to pull on her boots and retrieved her stick from where it leaned against the wall close to the lowest steps. Hester used it to push herself up to a standing position and made her way towards the door. She lifted her thick winter cape from its hook and engulfed herself in its warmth. Hearing Pa's mellow voice in the bedchamber above, Hester lifted the door latch and stepped outside.

She stared up and down the street. Wisps of orange light flickered behind ill-fitting shutters as neighbours roused themselves from slumber and stoked their cooking fires. Cockerels crowed with the break of dawn, and snuffling animal sounds came from backyards. The air was still, thin and frigid, with ribbons of fragrant woodsmoke creeping towards the sky. A hoarfrost sparkled on the snow-covered ground. Hester shivered and pulled her cape tighter around her as she walked away from her home. It was a perfect morning for clearing her mind and making sense of her life.

Hester's stick cracked frozen patches of snow as she took tentative steps. Her boots crunched over icy shards, and small clouds of breath left her lips. One of her neighbours stepped into the street and greeted her as he passed, setting his armour rattling as he strode towards the fort.

With no destination in mind, Hester wandered from one street to another. She passed the small old houses from the first days of the colony, and the house Pa had built for Ma before they had wed. Then she wandered into the newest street, where the houses were larger and sturdier, built for the latest influx of Puritans who had fled religious persecution. One or two stood empty, their occupants having returned to England, either because they were disillusioned by life in the colony or to give their support to Cromwell's army and fight against the King.

Thoughts tumbled and collided in Hester's mind as she forced herself to acknowledge other people's greetings. She silently railed at Ma and Pa for keeping her heritage a secret. She thought about her birth mother and wondered if she had inherited any of her passions and habits. She wondered if they would have sounded the same if they had laughed together. Heat coursed through Hester's body despite the biting chill. Her feeling of not belonging was starting to make sense. She belonged to different parents than the ones she had known all her life. Hers were a woman who died giving birth and a man who had fled the same night. And to make it all so much worse, other people knew! Hot tears soaked Hester's cheeks as she tried to quell her grief, but the pain of loss weakened her, making her leg muscles tremble beneath the layers of her skirts.

After walking every street and climbing to the top of the hill, Hester stopped to catch her breath and take in the view. The town sprawled away from her as if it was flowing towards the sea, and it was bathed in a silvery pink light from the early morning sun. Hester watched people emerging from their homes, scurrying like beetles across the glistening ground. The sun crept higher, washing the sea with a golden hue as it climbed from beyond the horizon far away to the east. England lay to the east. So did the bones of Hester's dead mother. A great gulping sob racked Hester's body. Her mother would never murmur soothing words nor place a comforting arm around her. Hester's breathing grew rapid. Her pulse thrummed in her ears. She staggered towards a rough-hewn bench positioned beneath a tree, but her vision greyed before she reached it, and her legs gave way.

'Hester! Hester, let me help you.' It was a man's voice. Deep, familiar and full of kindness, but it sounded far away. 'Hester, can you hear me?'

Cool fingers tapped on her cheek. She tried to open her eyes, but her eyelids were too heavy.

'You'll catch your death lying on the ground.'

Then I would be with my mother.

Powerful arms engulfed her body. She felt herself being lifted through the air. With a concerted effort, she opened her eyes. Her muscles turned rigid.

'Adam Phillips, what are you doing? Lower me at once!'

Adam met her demand with a kind smile. 'I will when we get to the bench.'

As Hester settled on the seat, her cheeks burned with shame. 'What were you thinking, carrying me like that? What if someone saw you?'

'I was concerned, Hester. You ignored my greeting when I called out to you, and you seemed lost in melancholy thoughts. Then, when I saw you fall, I thought you had passed out. Are you unwell?' Adam put his fingertip under Hester's chin and turned her face towards him. 'You look pale.'

Hester batted his hand away. 'I'm always pale. I've had distressing news, that's all.'

'Your parents will be worried. Let me walk you home.'

Hester shook her head. 'No! My parents are the source of my sadness.'

Hester heard Adam catch his breath. 'How so?'

'Because they have confessed to me that I'm not their daughter at all.' Hester shuffled on the bench until she was facing Adam. Tears streamed down her cheeks and trickled onto her cape. 'Tell me again, Adam,' she said between gulping sobs. 'What did you hear the day you overheard a conversation about my actual mother? Tell me the truth.'

After a long moment of hesitation, Adam said, 'Your father and my mother were expressing their concerns about the dangers women face during childbirth. Your father mentioned that your own mother died after labouring with you.'

Hester hammered the ground with her walking stick, creating icy mud shards. 'I should have challenged them that day.'

'I'm so sorry, Hester.'

Hester turned her head to look at him. 'You knew it was the truth but allowed me to believe it was a lie!' Her stomach tightened in a knot. 'That mean boy also knew. When he said my parents did not want me, he was so close to the truth. I cannot help but wonder who else Pa might have told.' Hester took a shuddering breath and pressed the heels of her hands to her eyes. 'You should have made it clear to me, Adam.'

'It was not my place to tell.'

Hester tilted her head back and stared up at the sky. Thin strands of white cloud stretched across the expanse of pale blue. 'What do you know about me and my parents?' Hester said. 'Tell me everything you know.'

'I have nothing more to tell than has already been said. Did you ask your parents about your birth mother?'

'I challenged Ma about it. She said my mother died and my father said he could not raise me, and so they took me in.'

'They did what they thought was best for you.'

'But Adam, I found out by accident! They should not have kept it from me. I didn't believe you when you repeated the words you overheard, but I found my actual mother's details in Ma's delivery ledger.' Hester relayed the events of the previous two days while Adam listened in silence. She described finding the scanty details about Hester Twisselton and overhearing the argument between Ma and Pa. Hester's fury burned deep inside her during her retelling of events. Adam placed his hand over hers. As his warm skin pressed against her cold, stiff fingers, she realised she had forgotten her gloves.

'You know, you are one of the fortunate ones,' Adam said, stroking her skin. 'Count your blessings for what you have in your life. Don't dwell on what is missing.'

Hester pulled her hand out from his. 'I'm an orphan. I'm not a Trelawney at all.'

'Hester, I know this news has rent your heart in two, but you have parents who love and respect you. They have kept you in their home when they could have sent you to another household. Isn't your mother teaching you her craft, and your father teaching you some physick?'

'Yes, but that serves a purpose for them too, because they do not pay me a wage.'

'But are we not fortunate to learn from our parents? My youngest brother is preparing to leave home in the spring to become an apprentice with the blacksmith in Salem. My father already has two sons working for him. There's insufficient work for a third.'

Hester fell silent for a few long moments. 'I think my brother will move away when he's a year or two older, perhaps to Boston. My father says Sam is quick with numbers and has the makings of a good merchant.'

'There you are, then.'

Hester caught Shadow peeping out from beneath Adam's jerkin and sniffing the icy air. After a furtive glance in Hester's direction, the little squirrel retreated to the warmth of its makeshift nest. Adam adjusted the lace of his jerkin and then pulled his cloak tighter around him. 'Hester, you and I are the fortunate ones. We will move out of our homes at the moment of our choosing.' He lowered his voice. 'Did you know Annie Atkins is an orphan?'

Hester's eyes darted towards Adam. 'I didn't.'

Annie lived with a farmer and his family, and she only ever left the farm to attend the Sabbath services. She rarely spoke to anyone other than to acknowledge a greeting and often drew a rebuke or shove from her master for no apparent reason.

'She's not the only orphan to go to a farming family and work the land from dawn until dusk. They don't pay her, Hester. Her only rewards are the food in her belly and the tired clothes that the women in the family have discarded. There are plenty of others like Annie, too.'

Hester felt a pang of sympathy for Annie. 'Adam Phillips, is that the truth you speak? Orphans end up as little more than slaves?'

Adam's expression turned solemn. 'It grieves me to say that for many orphans it is the case. It's my wish that one day I'll rescue a child or two from such a pitiful fate.'

'How will you do that?'

Adam scooped up a handful of ice and threw it onto the frozen ground. It shattered into tiny pieces that sparkled in the wintry sun. 'As I sit here with you today, it's nothing but a dream. But it's a dream I hope to fulfil. I've noticed a growing trend for men to have horses, and I've heard that horses have become especially popular among the men of Boston. The horse population increases with every ship's arrival, and I predict that in the years to come, almost every household will possess one. My father has taught me how to care for their hooves and, of course, how to shoe them. I have learned to care for sick mules and oxen, and I intend to educate myself about horses. They are beautiful creatures but are not well cared for. That's something I intend to change. After all, healthy animals make better workers, much like healthy people. If I can build a reputation as a farrier and doctor of horses, I should be able to turn my dream into a good business.'

Hester rubbed the toe of her boot into the ground to loosen a pebble encased in ice. 'How would that help orphans?'

Adam smiled. 'I'll earn good money and have a

comfortable home that will welcome unfortunate children. I'll teach them to read and be quick with numbers, and the boys will learn my trade. The girls will also learn to read, and they will follow the wise counsel of their adoptive mother.'

Hester sensed Adam watching her as she bent to pick up the pebble. She wrapped her fingers around the smooth surface of the ice-cold stone. 'You do not know how it feels to discover you are an orphan or that your parents abandoned you.' Hester had a bitter edge to her voice. 'It's no simple matter to fill the void left behind by such a loss or rejection. Did you know my father fled after I was born?' She pointed to the boot that covered her deformed foot and ankle. 'No doubt because of this.'

'He might have had a different reason, Hester. You cannot make such an assumption.' Adam reached for her hand again. This time, Hester welcomed his touch.

Hester looked straight at Adam. 'I need to learn more about my father, but it's not as if I can ask him. Would you be willing to help me?'

'Of course. But I'm not sure what I can do.'

After a long pause, Hester said, 'I'll ask my parents to tell me more. Yesterday I was too distressed to discuss it, and it's a conversation that I know will upset them. I don't want them to think I'm ungrateful for the care and love they have given me.' She placed her hand over her heart. 'I must fill the void in here. My father would have had a reason for fleeing. A good reason, I'm sure of it, and I need to know what drove him to do it. I need to understand who I am and where I truly belong.' Hester let out a slow breath. 'If Ma and Pa can't tell me what I need to know, I'll have to learn some other way.' She rested her hand on top of Adam's. 'I can't tell you how glad I am that you understand my situation and that you will help me.'

CHAPTER 13

HALFWAY THROUGH EATING HER SUPPER, Hester lowered her spoon. 'What did my mother look like?' She fixed Ma with a challenging stare. 'You would have been with her for a considerable time, so you must remember something about her appearance.'

Ma appeared to struggle to swallow a mouthful of pottage. She took a small sip of ale and looked at Hester. Her expression was soft and kind, but her loving face added to Hester's pain. Ma was nothing but a substitute for the woman who should have raised her. Hester looked at the other family members seated around the table and felt more distant from them than she had ever felt before.

Pa placed his spoon on the table. 'Close your mouth, Samuel, you look like a startled fish.'

Samuel chuckled, but everyone else remained silent.

'He can't be as shocked as I am to discover I don't belong here,' Hester said with a bitter edge to her voice.

Martha reached for Hester's hand and clasped it in her warm fingers. 'You do belong here, sister.'

'We are not sisters.'

Hester tried to withdraw her hand from Martha's, but Martha tightened her grip.

'We are sisters in all but blood. We've grown up together and shared a bed for as long as I can remember, and we've shared our dreams, confided secrets and tended to one another when sick. Our blood has nothing to do with that.' Martha released Hester's hand and took a sip of ale. 'Only last week I was telling Mercy how I can tell you anything. She said she wished you were her sister. I'm glad to have you as mine.'

'You're just being kind, Martha.' Hester watched a fragrant curl of steam rise from her bowl. The flavour and scent of onion, ginger and rosemary usually stimulated her appetite. Today, they made her stomach turn. She pushed the bowl away so that the smell of its contents no longer reached her nose.

'Your sister is right, Hester.' Ma's voice was thick with anguish. 'You are as much a part of this family as Martha and Samuel. You always will be. I deeply regret withholding the truth about your birth. Believe me, Hester, I meant well.' She lowered her voice. 'I was certain it was for the best, but now I see I made a dreadful error of judgement. I pray you can forgive me.'

'So, tell me, what did my mother look like?'

Ma raised her eyebrows at Pa as if seeking his permission to continue.

Pa nodded. 'Hester has a right to know.'

Samuel shovelled a mouthful of pottage into his mouth while fixing his gaze on Ma, curiosity radiating from him like heat from a cooking fire.

Ma lowered her head and wiped her hands on her napkin. A grave expression settled on her face as she looked back at Hester. 'Would you prefer us to discuss this in private?'

Hester hesitated. Martha stroked the back of Hester's hand. The kind gesture brought a lump to Hester's throat. Martha was flighty and sometimes conceited, but she always knew when to show kindness. It would be nice to have the comfort of her presence while Hester learned about what happened when she was born. She glanced at Samuel. He was trying to look disinterested while he continued eating, but his movements were stilted as he tried to ensure he did not miss a word of the conversation.

'We can talk about it here.'

'Very well.' Ma took a deep breath. 'I shall start from the beginning.'

Martha shuffled her chair nearer to Hester's. She put a comforting arm around her and rested her hand on Hester's shoulder. Hester pressed her cheek against Martha's fingers to show gratitude for her support.

Ma cleared her throat. 'Your father arrived at our door in a state of panic. He said your mother had fallen, and that she was losing blood. I suspected the placenta had ripped, so it was a matter of urgency to deliver you.' Ma's eyes had a faraway look. 'When I first saw your mother, she was so pale. She had been in labour for a couple of hours, and I could see she had lost a lot of blood.'

'Caused by her fall?' Hester asked, imagining the scene.

'I believed so. Your father was in a terrible state. I sent

him to fetch the surgeon, but your mother was fading fast.'

A shiver passed through Hester's body. Her mother must have been terrified and in so much pain.

Ma fiddled with her napkin, twisting it one way and then the other. 'The surgeon came as fast as he could. He stopped the bleeding after we delivered you, but it was too late to save your mother's life. I held her fingers against your cheek and told her she had a baby girl.' Ma caught her breath. 'I swear a flicker of a smile quivered on her lips just before she passed.'

A sob racked Hester's body. Tears cascaded down her cheeks. Martha rubbed her back and told her she was sorry.

'What did she look like?' Hester asked. 'Do I resemble her at all?'

'Your mother was young,' Ma said. 'Of a similar age to you now. And you look so much like her, Hester. Her hair was much fairer, but her complexion was pale like yours. You share her slight build too.'

Ma fell silent. Hester tried to imagine her real mother holding her in her arms, stroking her forehead and cheeks with a delicate, loving touch. Her heart ached.

'And my father?'

'I don't remember him very well. He was angry, I remember that, but grief overcame him, I suppose. We never saw him again.'

'You can't remember anything about him?'

Hester saw Ma flinch. 'I was too worried about your mother to pay much heed to your father. I remember the colour of his hair. It was the same shade of brown as yours.'

Hester balled her hands into fists. 'I can't believe he didn't want me.'

'I don't think that's true.' Pa furrowed his brow. 'I suspect it was more the case that your father could not accept his wife had died and he would have to raise a child by himself.'

Hester found the explanation hard to accept. Everyone knew about the dangers of childbirth, so the possibility of losing his wife must have crossed his mind. Hester looked at Ma. 'Did you ever try to find him?'

'He knew where we lived, Hester.' Ma lowered her voice until it was almost too quiet to hear. 'He did not approach our door again.'

'Will you all please excuse me?' Hester forced herself to smile at Martha. 'I need time alone to think.'

Martha moved her chair away to give Hester room to stand.

'Where are you going?' Samuel asked. He used his fingertips to wipe dregs from his bowl and made a loud slurping noise as he licked his fingers.

Hester bristled. 'I'm going to sit by the fire for a few minutes to try to make sense of what I have learned.'

'Would you like me to sit with you?' Ma offered. 'In case there is more you wish to ask?'

'Do you have more to tell me?'

Ma shook her head.

'Then I would prefer to sit alone.'

Ma nodded and instructed Samuel to clear the table. Hester stoked the fire and then sat in Pa's favourite chair.

She stared, not blinking, into the flames, trying to envisage the events of her birth. She imagined a young woman of her age terrified of going into labour. Hester quickly pushed the image away, not wanting to imagine the suffering her mother endured. She still knew so little about her birth parents, and she knew nothing about their personalities or their ambitions and desires. A large log cracked open in the fire and glowed orange at its heart. The heat made Hester's eyes ache. She knew her father had run away, unable to contemplate a life without his wife. But why had he abandoned his daughter, his own flesh and blood? He had left her to an unknown fate and at the mercy of the midwife who had delivered her. Hester glared at her left boot. Had her deformity repulsed her father? Had he chosen to reject a child who would never run or dance? Anger gnawed at the pit of her stomach. It wasn't her fault! A loud pop came from the fire, followed by a flurry of sparks. No, her father could not have been that cruel! He must have found himself in an impossible position. He would have needed to work to provide for a child, but someone else would have had to look after the child while he was working. Of course, he would not have been able to raise a child alone. He had lost his wife in the most tragic of circumstances; therefore, it was under-standable that while he was in the depths of his grief, he would have believed it impossible to raise a little girl. For all Hester knew, her father had worked hard to improve his situation so that he could take her back when his circumstances allowed. She had left England when she was only three years old. What situation might he be in now? Perhaps he thought about her every day and yearned for a reconciliation. Hester glanced towards Ma and watched her wipe crumbs from the table. A new thought took root in Hester's mind – a thought that made her uncomfortable. Perhaps her father had wanted her back, but Ma and Pa had wanted to keep her. That was not a question Hester felt able to ask, but somehow she would learn the truth.

CHAPTER 14

HESTER RUMMAGED in Ma's delivery bag and eased her
fingers between folded linens until she felt the cool metal
handles of the scissors. She pulled them free and opened
the blades, ready to cut the cord. 'Where did my father
go, Ma?'

Ma was stooped forward, guiding the baby's head as it
emerged from its mother. Without lifting her head, she
replied, 'He set off for Boston at first light. There's a
young apothecary he hopes to persuade to come here.
There are enough people in Plimoth to warrant one.' She
swept her finger around the baby's neck to check the
umbilical cord and gave a soft sigh of relief. 'All clear.
Prepare for one more mighty push, Mistress Stanton.
Your child will soon be here.'

Mistress Stanton's mother pulled a clean sheet from a
pile on a chair, ready to receive and wrap the baby. She
stood beside her daughter, chattering about whether her
next grandchild would be a sweet little girl or a robust
little boy.

'I'm not asking about Pa,' Hester said. 'I'm asking about my real father.'

Mistress Stanton's mother widened her eyes. Her daughter paused in her puffing and moaning. Hester saw Ma's expression fall and watched her purse her lips. *Good*, Hester thought, with a smugness that surprised her. *Ma feels some of my pain*.

A heavy silence stifled the room, and the fire seemed to burn brighter in the hearth. The baby slithered onto Ma's lap but lay limp and not breathing. Ma checked the baby's nose and mouth and then blew gently across its lips. Hester wondered if the baby was waiting for Ma to answer before taking the first lungful of air, then chided herself for mocking the seriousness of the situation.

'Now please, Hester.' Ma's voice had a sharp edge to it.

Hester snipped the cord and watched Ma lay the baby across her forearm. She rubbed its back with her free hand, then rocked it back and forth. The baby made a small gasp, and a pink bloom crept into its cheeks. A deep breath followed and then the baby cried with all its might.

'Praise the Lord!' Mistress Stanton raised herself up onto her elbows to admire her newborn.

'A little boy,' Ma said. She handed the baby to his eager grandmother and returned to the foot of the bed to wait for the placenta to emerge.

Hester caught Mistress Stanton casting curious glances at Ma.

Ma gave Hester a frosty glare. 'We'll discuss your father on our way home. We'll talk more about your mother's passing too. It can't be easy for you to come to terms with the circumstances of your own birth and how you became a Trelawney.'

Mistress Stanton's mother murmured something. It sounded like, 'Ah, that makes sense.'

Hester pondered why she might say such a thing and realised that her mention of her natural father might have suggested Hester had been born out of wedlock. Hester stifled a giggle. The very thought would have inflicted intense humiliation on Ma, especially in this Puritan household. But her desire to giggle soon faded when she realised the meaning behind Ma's retort. She had made it clear to the two women that Hester's father had abandoned her and that Ma had given her a home.

Hester regretted discussing herself in another woman's house. It was bad enough they witnessed her limp without pitying her for the circumstances of her birth. She had also soured Ma's mood, which did not bode well for the rest of the day. Her flippant question about her father would not make further conversation easy.

Icy roads made the walk home treacherous, and the bitter air stung Hester's face. She was tired from sleepless nights spent imagining her father's reaction to her birth and then deciding to leave her. When she did drift off to sleep, she dreamed about her mother and how the poor young woman had lost her life before she could hold her daughter.

Hester's stick shot across a slick of ice. Ma grabbed her arm to keep her upright. 'Link your arm through mine,

Hester. I can't have you landing on your bottom and making another scene.'

'I'm sorry, Ma.' Hester scrutinised the frozen ground, hunting for more slippery patches.

'For the life of me, I don't know why you did that! It's no one's business but ours.'

'I said I'm sorry.' Prickly heat irritated Hester's neck despite the January air. 'Ma,' Hester said tentatively, 'do you think my father still lives in London? Do you think he wonders where I am?'

Hester felt Ma's arm stiffen. 'Perhaps, Hester. But remember, in the three years before we moved here, he did not return to our door.'

A knot tightened in Hester's stomach. 'There's so much I want to know.'

'Sometimes, it's a blessing to not know everything.' Ma softened her tone. 'The truth is not always kind.'

'But my parents were the reason for my being. It's because of them that I came into this world. I have their blood flowing through my veins, but I know next to nothing about them.'

Hester tried to picture her parents and imagined a young couple sitting by a fire, the woman nearing the end of her pregnancy. They would have discussed whether their baby would be a boy or a girl. They would have chosen names. 'Ma, do you remember their home?'

Ma slowed her pace but said nothing.

'Do you?'

'I'm trying to recall.' Ma thought for a moment. 'It wasn't large, but it was clean, and your mother had prepared for your arrival. She had even prepared a pot of hot water before she took to her bed.'

Hester found it comforting that her mother had looked forward to giving birth to her. 'Did they live in a decent neighbourhood? What did my father do for work?'

Ma tightened her grip on Hester's arm but did not return her smile. 'I'm sorry, Hester, I don't remember. I set foot in that home over eighteen years ago and have entered many hundreds of others since. One memory blurs with another.'

They completed their walk home in silence, apart from to return the greeting of a neighbour as they passed her in the street. Hester offered to write the delivery notes in the ledger, and Ma accepted without protest. Hester doubted Ma would ever protest again now that she had discovered her secret.

After entering the details of young Master Stanton's birth, Hester flipped the pages back to the details of her own birth. The lack of information was more striking than before. It also seemed intentional.

Hester cleaned her quill and placed the stopper in the ink bottle while listening for telltale sounds of who was at home. Martha's agitated voice drifted from the stillroom, and Hester heard Ma's calming reply. Pa was still in Boston, and there were no grunts, snorts or scrapes to suggest Samuel was somewhere in the house. Hester closed the delivery ledger and returned it to its place on the shelf. Then she hobbled into the small room her father used to consult with his patients. There was a large wooden trunk beside his writing desk, and Hester knew it was full of papers. If he had any correspondence referring to her father, she was certain she would find it there.

Most of the documents were old medical journals and patient records. There were also receipts for a pestle and mortar, oils, minerals and herbs. There were several letters from a surgeon named Giles Heale, a friend of Pa's who lived in London. He wrote to her father several times a year, keeping him abreast of events in England and describing new trends in medical and surgical practice. Hester had a dim memory of spending time with him and his wife when she was very little. They had cared for her from time to time when Ma and Pa were both busy with patients. Hester's heart beat harder in her chest. Was he the surgeon who delivered her? Might he know more about her parents? Hester resumed studying the letters with more vigour, searching for clues. She put aside all the letters signed by Giles and hunted for a mention of the Twisselton name. By the time she had looked through every letter in the chest, papers lay strewn around her, but she was still none the wiser about why her father had never claimed her. Had he really run away and abandoned his newborn daughter? Or had he fled after her mother's death to avoid an almighty scandal? Hester knew Pa had treated men of the royal court – she had seen letters gushing with their gratitude. Perhaps her real father was a man of power, and her mother had been his mistress. Such a man might go to great lengths to conceal a secret lovechild.

'Hester!'

She spun around to see Ma staring wide-eyed at the mess of papers.

Hester used the desk to pull herself up from the floor. Grief gripped her hard in the chest and took away her breath. 'There's nothing here.' She gave in to the tears she had been struggling to suppress. Her body convulsed with sobs. 'There's no trace of my mother and father.'

Ma hurried across to Hester and engulfed her in her arms. 'My darling girl, I'm so sorry.'

Hester returned Ma's embrace and clung to her. 'I have nothing from my parents! No memories, no letters. Nothing at all!'

Ma's cool hand stroked Hester's cheeks, brushing away hot tears. 'You're wrong, Hester. You have your mother in your heart and blood. And you have her name.'

'Did she choose it for me?' Hester asked between great choking sobs.

Ma shook her head. 'No, Hester, I did.'

Hester eased herself out of the embrace. To have her mother's name was a comfort, but Hester wished her own mother had named her. And she could not shed the niggling doubt that Ma was still keeping something from her.

CHAPTER 15

'You stay at home today.' Ma piled fresh linen into her delivery bag and gathered a shawl and cloak ready to venture outdoors. Freezing temperatures had kept a thick coating of snow over the town, and even though the end of February approached, there was still no sign of an imminent thaw. 'Let the heat of the fire ease your pain. There are a few shirts in need of mending. You could make a start on those.'

'No, Ma.' Hester's pain was always worse with the bitter chill of winter. She eased her left foot into her boot, grimacing as her skin caught the seam over one of the metal support rods. The blister she had developed months earlier had only recently healed, and the fragile new skin was still tender. 'I'd rather accompany you, and I should very much like to deliver Mistress Pooley's child. I'll work on the shirts later.'

Ma smiled and placed her cool hand on Hester's cheek. 'You have the makings of an excellent midwife, Hester. I've seen you studying my notes.'

Hester felt her cheeks glow. It was rare for Ma to praise her so. Hester was confident that she could handle most situations without panicking, but she needed more experience to prove that to herself. She knew that in the other colonies, women often delivered each other's babies and only called the midwife if there was a problem. But here in Plimoth the women preferred the reassurance and expertise of the midwife and her daughter. "Her daughter". How Hester loved the sound of that! After a few hard weeks of coming to terms with her past, Hester had shifted her attitude and was content to think of herself as "The Chosen One". The name that Weetamoo had given to Hester was a simple statement of fact. Ma could have left Hester to an uncertain fate but had taken her home instead.

The Pooleys' house was near the blacksmith's forge, and Hester hoped for a glimpse of Adam. She had not seen him for several weeks and missed the warmth of his companionship. Her heart sank a little when she noticed the forge fire had burned low and Adam was nowhere to be seen. She imagined him working on one of the remote farms, applying a poultice to an ox's sore leg while his father fitted shoes to a horse.

'Mistress Trelawney! Praise the Good Lord, you're here.' A grim-faced woman met Ma at the door. She nodded an acknowledgement to Hester. 'Thank ye both for coming.' She jerked her head towards the interior of the small house. 'She pays no heed to me even though we're the closest of friends. 'Tis a sorry situation she's in.' The woman wrung her hands on a stained apron. 'You'd better hurry on in.'

Ma stepped aside for Hester to enter first. Hester's pulse quickened as she appraised the situation. Mistress Pooley lay exhausted on a crude wooden bed, the mattress old and tatty with straw leaking from the seams. Her skin was ghostly pale and she reeked of stale sweat. Her lips were pinched together and her eyes had a look of fear.

'Mistress Pooley, I'm Hester Trelawney.' Hester reached for her hand and gave it a reassuring squeeze. 'My mother, Desire, is here too. May I look underneath the sheet to check on the babe's progress?'

Mistress Pooley turned her head away. 'Do what you must.'

Hester released her hand. She took a steadying breath and lifted the sheet. She had expected to see a large pool of blood but found nothing untoward. The blood loss was minimal, and the baby's head was partway out between Mistress Pooley's legs.

'Your baby's ready to be born,' Hester said, feeling the tension ebb from her neck and shoulders. 'You must take a deep breath and prepare to push.'

'I can't,' came a feeble reply.

'You must! This baby is almost here. He or she needs your help.'

Mistress Pooley's face contorted. 'I told you, I can't.'

Hester had not encountered such resistance before. 'You'll feel an urge to push when you have the next contraction. A few strong pushes and your baby will be out.'

Ma tapped Hester on the shoulder to let her know she had placed a stool behind her. Hester was relieved to take the weight off her foot and settled herself to deliver the baby.

'Come now, Mistress Pooley,' Hester said. 'I know you can do it.'

Mistress Pooley made a lowing sound as a strong contraction gripped her womb. Her urge to push took over, and she followed Hester's instructions.

The delivery proceeded without complications, and the newborn little girl was quick to give a mewling cry. Hester handed her to Ma for wiping and wrapping, but when Ma tried to hand the baby to her mother, Mistress Pooley refused to take her.

Hester stood to admire the bundle nestled in Ma's arms. 'Mistress Pooley, you have a beautiful daughter,' she said.

Mistress Pooley ignored Hester and screwed her eyelids shut. A tear trickled down her cheek.

'Mistress Pooley—'

'Let her have a moment, Hester,' Ma said, taking her arm and drawing her away from the bed. 'Some new mothers need a little time to adjust. Childbirth can be overwhelming.'

Hester settled back on the stool to deliver the placenta. She checked for tears and, satisfied it was intact, she put the placenta in a bowl ready for burning. She cleaned and tidied around Mistress Pooley and settled her on a clean sheet. After helping her to sit up on her bed, she said, 'It's time to meet your daughter.'

'It's best if I don't.'

A chill rippled through Hester. 'Why?'

Mistress Pooley's shoulders twitched, and she started

sobbing. 'I can't raise her by myself, so I'll have to give her away.'

Hester regarded the bundle nestled in Ma's arms. A tiny girl with dainty little hands and two perfect feet. Her chill turned to anger. 'God's blood, woman, why would you do that?'

'Hester.' Ma's sharp tone struck Hester like a slap. 'We will leave Mistress Pooley with her neighbour.'

Chastened, Hester loaded her scissors and unused linens into the delivery bag and retrieved her walking stick from the corner of the room. She stopped by the door and turned back towards Mistress Pooley. 'Please forgive me,' she said. 'I believe I spoke out of turn.'

The neighbour sidled up to Hester and spoke in a lowered voice. 'Her husband upped and left three days ago. Said he'd had enough of working the land and fancied a life at sea. I knew he was a bad 'un the moment I met him.' She gazed fondly at Mistress Pooley. 'She's a good 'un though. Can't do enough for me and my little 'uns. So don't you go worrying, my dear. Me and my husband, we have little to give, but we'll see she's looked after, and her baby. One look at that little beauty and she'll be smitten.'

The neighbour's kindness brought a lump to Hester's throat. The absent Master Pooley cared nothing for his child and had not thought twice about abandoning his wife. At least the child would have a home with this kind neighbour until Mistress Pooley had a change of heart.

'I'll tell you somethin' else, too.' The neighbour chuckled. 'Her husband ain't cut out for a life at sea. I wager he'll be back afore the summer.'

Ma wrapped Hester's cloak around her shoulders. 'Come, Hester. Your work here is done.'

The neighbour pressed a small earthenware pot into Hester's hand. 'Honey,' she said. 'You'll not find a tastier sample than that. We'll get your payment to you as soon as we can.'

Hester tightened her grip on the pot. 'Your kindness is payment enough today.' She nodded to the swell beneath the neighbour's skirt. 'Perhaps next time, I'll charge a little more.'

The neighbour smiled. 'That sounds like a grand arrangement to me.'

CHAPTER 16

Rain washed away the last of the snow, and spring brought colour to the landscape. Trees unfurled glossy green leaves, and wood anemones dotted the hedgerows with splashes of white and pink. The air was warm against Hester's skin and sweet blooms scented the air. Spring was Hester's favourite time of year, but its arrival did little to calm her anguish. Nightmares gave her broken sleep because of recurring dreams about her father. Every morning she struggled to rise, swamped in a blanket of fatigue and feeling ever more unsettled.

Hester climbed the hill towards the mill, following the brook and scanning the water for a silver flash of a herring. Her mood lifted as she glimpsed one darting through the shallows. She took deep breaths of fresh clean air and tried to quicken her pace. The gentle babble of the brook gave way to the thunderous sounds of the mill's wheel churning through the water. Hester knocked on the solid wooden door that opened onto the grinding floor of the mill. A woman's voice called for her to enter.

'Good morrow, Widow Jenney.' Hester removed her felt hat and smiled.

Widow Jenney paused in her sweeping and beamed at her. 'Hester! 'Tis always a pleasure to see you.' The exertion with the broom had left her a little breathless and caused her cheeks to redden. She rested her broom against a large wooden hopper.

Hester looked around the room. Sunlight streamed through a window, making the air sparkle with fragments of corn dust. 'Is all well here?' she asked, surprised to see the grinding stone lying still.

Widow Jenney nodded towards a set of stairs leading to a lower floor. 'Simon's checking the gears while we're not busy.' Her smile faded. 'My husband, God rest his soul, always said we should fix things before problems occur. Simon is determined to follow his father's example and keep our mill's good name. Rumours are rife that a miller from Boston might settle in this town, so we need to do all we can to keep the milling to ourselves.' Her expression lightened again. 'Come to the house, my dear. I have a pitcher of small beer to quench our thirsts while you attend to my arm.'

The widow's home was small and cluttered but welcoming and clean. Her table gleamed with a coat of wax polish, and there were soft cushions on the benches and chairs. A bowl of fragrant dried flower petals sat at the centre of the table, and lavender sprigs by the windows infused the air with their scent. Hester spotted a man's wide-brimmed hat dangling from a hook by the door. She wondered if it had belonged to Miller Jenney and if his widow kept it where it had always been to keep the memory of her husband alive.

The widow poured them each a cup of beer before perching on a bench she had pulled out from beneath the table. Hester propped her walking stick against the wall and then sat beside the widow.

'How is your arm today?' Hester asked, struggling to stifle a yawn.

'Better, I think. Still sore, but not as painful as it was.'

Hester pushed one of Widow Jenney's linen sleeves up her arm. Next, she loosened the thin strip of fabric she had used to protect the wound caused by Widow Jenney burning her skin on a hot metal cauldron.

'It's not as angry today,' Hester said, after easing off the poultice and wiping away remnants of salve with gentle sweeps of the bandage cloth. She traced her finger around the edge of the wound. The skin was still a little too warm but not as hot and angry as it had been. Hester reached into her basket and lifted out a glass bottle stoppered with a piece of stone wedged into place with a scrap of rag. She pulled the rag to ease out the stone and released a sharp tang of vinegar from the neck of the bottle. It caused a tingle up Hester's nose, and the odour was so pungent it burned at the back of her throat. 'My pa said I should use this to clean the wound before I apply more honey salve.'

Hester took a clean piece of linen from her bag and soaked it with vinegar, then dabbed at the widow's healing wound. Widow Jenney let out a yelp when Hester cleaned a raw patch near the centre. 'Forgive me,' she said, dabbing again. 'This will prevent an infection.'

She looked up to meet the widow's gaze. Her eyes

were moist from smarting with pain, but she gave Hester a grateful smile.

'There's something special about your gentle touch, Hester. You have the gift of healing at your fingertips.'

They both laughed.

'You didn't need me for this,' Hester said. 'You could have done it yourself.'

Widow Jenney patted Hester's hand. 'I wouldn't do it so well. And anyway, I enjoy your company for the few minutes we share.'

'As do I.' Hester took a few sips of nutty beer, relishing the cool liquid on her tongue. *This is who I am*, thought Hester. *The youngest midwife in the colony, a competent nurse and a friendly neighbour*. The idea gave her a warming rush of contentment.

Widow Jenney waited for Hester to finish cleaning the wound and re-dressing the burn before saying, 'Did you hear the news about the blacksmith?'

Hester shook her head. 'Nothing scandalous, I hope.'

'Oh, goodness me, no. Nothing of that nature. The poor man had a pain in his chest last night and thought it was from rushing his supper. He retired early for the night, hoping it would ease, but when his wife went to check on him a few minutes later, her dear husband... well, he was...' Her voice faded. She lowered her head.

A chill rippled down Hester's spine. 'He passed?' Hester found it hard to accept. He had looked so well the last time she saw him. 'He always appeared so hale and hearty,' she said.

Widow Jenney gave a small shrug. 'It was the same for

my John.' She sighed. 'His poor widow. I know how hard it will be for her in the weeks ahead.'

Hester's thoughts turned to Adam. He would be mourning his father, and she understood the pain of such a loss. She replaced the vinegar and salve in her basket and took a mouthful of beer. 'Forgive me, Mistress Jenney, but I must leave you now. Ma will be wondering what's taking me so long.' She looped the handle of her basket over her arm. 'I'll pass by the forge on my way home and offer my condolences to the blacksmith's family.'

It was only a short walk to the blacksmith's house. Hester found Adam sitting outdoors, his face buried in his hands.

'Adam,' she said softly. 'I'm so sorry about your father's passing. If there's anything I can do…'

'I wish you could bring him back,' he said.

'If I could, I would, I assure you,' Hester replied, thinking that she would bring her mother back too.

Adam raised his head. Grey shadows rimmed his eyes. 'Will you sit with me for a moment? My mother has taken to her bed and cannot speak for grief.'

'Does she have someone with her?'

'My sister.'

A movement inside Adam's jacket betrayed Shadow's presence. Adam lifted the squirrel out and held it to his chest. The squirrel fixed its gaze on Hester, as if waiting for her to speak, but Hester could find nothing to say. She settled beside Adam on the bench, and they sat together in silence. Something grey caught Hester's eye as it shook a section of hedgerow. A young rabbit emerged onto the grass and twitched its tiny nose. It surveyed its surroundings before hopping towards a clump of white crocuses.

'I wonder where its home is,' Hester said, watching the rabbit disappear back into the greenery. Under her breath, she added, 'I wonder where my real home is too.'

'What did you say?' Adam returned Shadow to the safety of his jerkin and then rubbed his eyes. When he looked at Hester, his eyes had turned pink from his attempts to erase his grief.

Hester reached for Adam's hand and squeezed his fingers. 'Nothing important. Widow Jenney sends her condolences. Will you tell your mother?'

Adam nodded and released Hester's hand. 'If you will excuse me, I think I'll tell her now.'

Hester watched him walk away, weighed down by his mourning. She had failed to ease his grief, but she could ease her own feeling of emptiness. Her father, as far as she knew, was still alive and living in England. She turned her attention towards the sea, the ocean that kept them apart. She would try to find her father and make sense of who she was.

CHAPTER 17

APRIL ARRIVED with light showers and heavy grey clouds that cleared away by noon. The afternoon sun warmed Hester's back as she shuffled along the edge of the herb bed, kneeling to pull out weeds. It was a task she found much easier to do while the rain-soaked earth was soft.

A commotion behind her set the chickens squawking. Hester peered over her shoulder and saw Ma rushing towards Pa with a letter in her hand.

'It's from Giles,' Ma said.

Hester grasped her walking stick and scrambled to her feet, eager to hear the latest news from England.

Pa abandoned his attempts to repair a hole in the chicken house roof and brushed dust from his breeches. 'It's a little soon for a letter from Giles. I hope it's not bad tidings.' Pa broke the seal and scanned the contents. Letters from Pa's surgeon friend always brought a smile to his lips, but something in this letter had left him crestfallen instead.

'Is it the war?' Hester asked, trying to brush off damp

soil that clung to her skirt. 'Does your friend have to fight?'

'No, it's not that.'

'What does he say, Jed?' Pa's reaction to the letter had put a brittleness into Ma's voice.

Pa looked at the letter again. 'He said the Civil War continues with victory likely to favour the Roundheads. Cromwell has appointed a captain general to train his New Model Army, and it has the organisation and funding needed to defeat the King's Cavaliers. How long it will take for a decisive victory, he cannot say.' Pa used his shirtsleeve to wipe beads of sweat from his brow. 'Giles says he has a lawsuit rumbling on – some dispute or other over an unpaid invoice. He doesn't wish to bore us with the details. He mentions it only to defer painful news.'

Pa lowered the letter. His eyes were glistening, and Hester wondered what terrible news might cause Pa to cry.

'What else does he say?' Hester asked.

Pa reached for Ma's hand before answering. 'The Good Lord has seen fit to take our beloved friend, Mary.'

'No!' Ma pressed her fist to her mouth. 'Dear Mary! Had she been unwell?'

Pa shook his head. 'Her passing was sudden. Giles says his brother and sister-in-law stayed with him for six weeks to help him through his grief. It is only now that he feels able to share the news that he has lost his one great love.' Pa raised his hand to shield his face from the sun as he stared towards the bay. 'There's a ship leaving the harbour later today. I'll send a letter with our condolences.'

Pa strode towards the house, leaving Hester and Ma to tidy away his tools.

'I'm sorry for your loss, Ma,' Hester said, stacking a pile of small wooden slats. 'I know you were fond of Mary.' She almost put an arm around Ma, but something held her back.

'Thank you, Hester.' Ma stood upright. Both her cheeks were damp.

Hester had a clean linen square tucked into her sleeve. She pulled it out and gave it to Ma.

'Do you remember Mary and Giles?' Ma asked, dabbing her face with the linen.

Hester tried to conjure their images in her mind. She recalled a man with a kind face, a gentle voice and a neat beard, but she could remember nothing of Mary. 'Not really,' she said.

'Of course you don't. I was daft to ask. You were so little when we left.' Ma took a deep breath. 'Weeping won't bring Mary back. How are you getting on with the weeds?'

'Almost finished.'

'Good. I think I might take the boat to Duxbury this afternoon to visit the General Store. Several of our neighbours are going. Would you like to come too?'

'Yes, Ma. I would love to.'

Ma smiled. 'If we're lucky, Standish will have fresh supplies of sugar, spices and raisins.' She turned to walk away.

After a moment's hesitation, Hester called out to her. 'Ma? Was Giles the surgeon you sent for to attend to my mother?'

Ma stopped walking and stood still, her back towards Hester. She turned around, her expression taut. 'Yes, Hester, he was.'

Hester's heart skipped a beat. 'Why did you never say so before?'

Ma shrugged and looked away. 'There was no need to mention it.'

Hester tightened her grip on her walking stick and gazed towards Plimoth harbour, where cartloads of beaver and otter pelts lined a section of beach. Crewmen bustled back and forth, yelling to one another. Some were loading pelts onto tenders while others stacked barrels and crates. The sound of wood smacking against wood echoed in Hester's ears. In a matter of hours, the ship would set sail with Pa's letter to Giles. Hester felt her heartbeat quicken. The surgeon had saved her life the day she was born, and because he was her father's friend, he might agree to help her again.

By the time the shallop set sail from Plimoth, it was packed with eager shoppers. Hester sat pressed against Ma on one side and the gunwale on the other. Someone nearby smelt unwashed, and the pungent smell made Hester's nostrils sting. She shuffled and twisted on the bench seat until she faced the sea, relishing a blast of clean, briny air. The shallop caught a small wave and showered Hester with tiny droplets, but the cool spray did little to distract her from the thoughts tumbling through her mind. She could not stop thinking about Giles Heale and his presence at her birth. He might remember her parents' home and recall why her father fled.

The shallop jolted as it ran aground on the beach, stirring Hester out of her reverie. She tried to dismiss all thoughts of the surgeon as she followed Ma to Standish's store. Cabinets and shelves filled the shop, displaying a variety of wares. The air was heavy with the scents of perfumes, spices and musty bolts of wool cloth. Hester scanned the shelves laden with small bulging sacks, glass bottles and earthenware jars but felt no inclination to read the labels or remove stoppers to sniff their contents. She watched Ma fill a basket with candles and another with linen, buttons and laces, then left her to finish her shopping alone while she perused a few shelves and cabinets.

Hester found herself drawn towards a corner of the store where a cabinet displayed quills, blocks of wax and a few small pots of ink. On one shelf there were journals bound in leather jackets, and two piles of loose paper with sheets of different sizes. Hester took out a quill. The feather was longer than most quills, and it was glossy and black. The shaft was already cut and shaped and looked as if it would hold the perfect amount of ink without causing unsightly blotches. She imagined herself using it to write notes in Ma's ledger. Regretting she had left her coins at home, Hester returned the quill to the shelf. They had a few good quills at home, but nothing as exquisite.

The shallop hummed with joyful chatter all the way back to Plimoth. Mothers and daughters planned to cook stews flavoured with pepper and thyme, or bake cakes sweetened with sugar and crammed with juicy raisins. As Ma talked to her neighbour about making rabbit stew spiced with cinnamon and nutmeg, Hester's thoughts drifted to the cabinet of quills, paper and ink. She could not help but wonder whether Pa's friend would reply to a letter if she was brave enough to send one? And more importantly, would he share his memories of her father?

CHAPTER 18

HESTER HELPED Ma unload her purchases and stow them in the kitchen and stillroom. Afterwards, she settled in a chair by the window and stitched a seam that was fraying on one of Samuel's old shirts. Watching the needle move in and out through the fine fabric, Hester allowed her thoughts to wander. She considered the words she might use in a letter to the surgeon. Then she imagined writing another letter that she would address to her father – a letter that might lead to a reunion. Hester imagined a tearful reconciliation where her father would express deep regret for not finding her sooner. They would talk late into the night, learning about each other's lives and forging an emotional connection. She imagined it would be difficult at first, while they remained uncertain of each other, but after a little awkwardness, it would feel as if they had never been apart. They would discuss her mother, her habits and mannerisms, and the meals she liked to cook. Her father would reminisce about her mother's favourite colours and the songs she sang while she worked. Hester would ask about her mother's favourite scent. Was it lavender, jasmine, or orange flowers? Or had she shared Ma's preference for the sweet floral perfume of rose? Hester's eyes misted over, blurring the needle as it pierced the shirt and causing her to prick her skin.

'Ouch!'

'Hester?'

'It's nothing, Ma.' A bead of blood touched the linen and crept through the fibres. Hester sucked her bleeding finger and chastised herself for not paying more attention. She would have to remove the stain by soaking the linen in a bucket of salted water.

'Are you weeping?'

Hester blotted her eyes with the back of her hand. 'No, Ma, I pricked myself. The needle went under my fingernail.'

Ma pulled a face. 'I sometimes do that myself. Here, pass the shirt to me.'

'No, I'll do it.' Hester sucked her finger again to remove another bead of blood. 'I've almost finished. Shall I mend Pa's cape next?'

Ma shook her head. 'Leave it until another day. It makes your father look like a ghoul in a shroud. I do wish he'd stop wearing it.'

He's not my real father. The thought struck Hester hard and took her breath away. She tightened her grip on Samuel's shirt and took a moment to compose herself. 'Pa worked hard for that cape, Ma. And everyone knows the physician is on his way when they glimpse his black silhouette in the distance.'

Ma reached into the basket and stroked the fabric of the cape. 'He was so proud the day he first wore it, but the repair can wait.'

Hester resumed her stitching, taking care to avoid stabbing herself again. Her thoughts returned to her father. She wondered if he had remarried, and if he had a kind wife. She imagined looking in a mirror with a younger half-sister, admiring the similar shapes of their noses and identical colouring of their eyes. How old would her sister be? Sixteen, like Martha? If so, they could explore London's streets together and peer through shop windows or buy trinkets from market stalls. They might even visit the theatre and watch one of William Shakespeare's plays, then scurry from the paths of carriages rolling along narrow streets. They would visit a cordwainer's shop together and order a pair of dainty shoes and an elegant pair of boots.

Hester tied off her stitching and snapped off the thread. As she checked the neatness of the repair, she formed a simple plan. The next time she found herself alone at home, she would put pen to paper. She would write a letter to her father and share her yearning to see him. She would also write to Giles Heale and ask him if he could find a way to forward her letter to her father.

Hester did not want Ma and Pa to know about her plan. They had kept their secret from her for years; it was time for a secret of her own.

CHAPTER 19

FOUR DAYS PASSED before Hester found herself alone in the house. Ma and Pa had left early that morning to visit the Aldens in Duxbury and had taken Samuel with them. Martha was at the Bradfords' house, where she and Mercy shared a large buck tub in which to do the weekly laundry for the two families. After milking both goats and collecting the fresh eggs, Hester peeled and chopped some onions, then skinned and chopped up two rabbits. She stripped the leaves from sprigs of thyme and parsley and added her ingredients to a large cauldron simmering by the fire. Next, she worked on the dough Ma had started before departing for Duxbury. Hester separated the dough into small rounds and set them aside to rise before she baked them a little later. With all her chores completed for the morning, Hester set about finding some paper on which to write to her father and Giles Heale.

Hester scoured Pa's office for his writing materials. She found his wax seal, quills and ink stowed in a drawer, but he had used the last of his paper to send his condolences to his friend. Hester pursed her lips as she scanned the shelves for something she could use instead. Most of the books were printed texts or ledgers of accounts. She ran her fingertips across the spines and came to Pa's patient ledgers. Hester carried them to the writing desk and flicked through the pages. One was full, the other almost full, and the third had entries on the first twelve pages. Hester checked the date of the last entry in the second ledger. 'The eighth day of the seventh month in the year of our Lord 1645,' Hester said aloud. Almost nine months earlier. Pa had started a new ledger before filling that one. He was unlikely to use it again. Without hesitation, Hester ripped out two of the blank pages. She helped herself to Pa's quills and ink and settled at the parlour table to write.

Several minutes passed. Both sheets of paper remained untouched. What should she say to a man she didn't know? How should she introduce herself? Whatever details she shared, she must not sound too needy. If she portrayed herself in a pleasing manner, her father would be eager to reply. She tapped her lip with the end of the quill, feeling the barbs tickle her skin. The letter would not write itself, so she dipped the nib in ink.

Dear Father,

Hester studied her handwriting. The letters were neat enough, but the greeting was wrong. A familial greeting might shock her father and cloud his reaction to the rest of her letter. She needed to think of something more formal. She moved her hand lower down the page and started writing again.

Dear Master Twisselton,

Please forgive the unexpected arrival of this letter, and any surprises it might contain. I have only recently learned of your existence and thought you might be glad to hear from me. It will please you to know that I am well, living in the Plimoth Colony in Massachusetts. I arrived here when I was three years old. You might remember my adoptive mother, Desire Trelawney. She was the midwife who attended my mother on the day that I was born.

The sound of the door latch lifting set Hester's pulse racing. She twisted on the seat, holding her breath, waiting to see who would come in.

'Ma!'

'I had to curtail my visit to the Aldens. Elenor Pearce is in labour, so I need my delivery bag.' Ma approached the table with her head cocked a little to one side. 'What are you doing?'

Hester's mouth dried, and her tongue seemed to stick in her throat. 'I was trying to... I thought I'd...' Hester turned to look at the paper on the desk. She turned it over and laid the quill across it. 'I thought I would make brief notes about the recent deliveries I have attended. I thought it might be a good idea to start my own records.' *Dear God, forgive me for lying,* she thought, *but the truth would break Ma's heart.*

Ma nodded her approval. 'Excellent idea. Do that later and come with me now. Elenor's birth will be something noteworthy. I'm certain she's expecting twins.'

Twins! Hester had never seen twins being born. *But what about my letters?* Hester's thoughts flew back and forth as she struggled to decide. The yearning to contact her real father outweighed the desire to see the twins. She massaged her temples with her fingertips. 'I'm feeling awful poorly, Ma. I think I might need to lie down.'

Ma's face dropped, and she placed the back of her hand across Hester's brow. 'Praise the Lord, you have no fever.' She glanced at the blank piece of paper covered by the quill.

Hester grasped the edge of the paper as if she would turn it over. Instead, she held it still. 'I'll write my notes later,' she said, pulling a mournful expression. 'Shall I join you after I've rested?'

'Better not, Hester.' Ma looked disappointed. ''Tis a shame to hear myself turn you down. But if you are sickening for something, we can't have you at the birth.' Ma narrowed her eyes. 'This isn't like you, Hester. It would be more usual for you to feign good health rather than miss an opportunity like this.'

Hester fought to hold her nerve under Ma's intense scrutiny. Her stomach did a little flip, and bile burned the back of her throat. 'I'm a little queasy, Ma. I worry I might be sick.'

Ma widened her eyes. 'You have turned a little pale.' She planted a kiss on Hester's forehead. 'I hope you recover soon, my love.'

Hester watched Ma scoop up her delivery bag and hurry out of the house. She could not deny a little regret at missing the birth of twins, but having time at home alone would allow her to write her letters. Hester read the words she had written and considered starting again. She had failed to mention that she was Master Twisselton's daughter. After several minutes of procrastination, Hester continued from where she had left off.

I am your daughter, Master Twisselton, and the midwife named me Hester in honour of my mother, your beloved deceased wife.

Hester paused again. He would remember her deformity. She must reassure him it caused her little strife.

You might recall that I was born with a misshapen left foot. It causes me very little bother provided I wear supportive boots. I use a walking stick when I am out of doors, but I manage all of my daily chores with no difficulty whatsoever.

Hester wondered what else she should say. How much should she write in the letter? How much should she keep until they met? They had so many years to catch up on. She decided it best to keep the letter brief.

It would bring me great happiness if you would reply to this letter. It would please me even more to learn that you share my wish to meet.

May the Lord bless you and keep you safe.

Yours,

Hester

Hester folded the top of the paper just below her abandoned start and used a knife to tear it away, leaving a neat edge. She threw the unwanted piece of paper onto the fire and watched it curl, blacken and burn. She read through her letter one more time before folding it and applying a seal. Next, she had to write to Giles Heale. She took the other page she had torn from the ledger. This time the words flowed more easily.

Dear Master Heale,

First, please accept my condolences. Although I do not remember Mary, I know both she and you showed kindness to me when I was a very young child. I hope the pain of your grief is easing — I know how a loss can be difficult to bear.

I have also experienced recent grief. Please do not let this revelation alarm you — my ma and pa are both well! My grief ensued after learning about the circumstances of my birth and my natural mother's passing. I still find it difficult to understand what happened and why I have no contact with my father. I wonder if he ever thinks of me, or, indeed, if he has been trying to find me.

I wish to locate my real father, and I am hoping you will help. Ma says she cannot recall the neighbourhood where I was born, nor the name of the street. I wonder if you can. As you still live in London, familiarity with the neighbourhoods might help you recall — it was a rather dramatic event according to my ma's account.

If you can recall the address, or better still, possess knowledge of my father's whereabouts, please will you forward the enclosed letter to him? It will then be for him to decide what to do with the information I have shared.

I beg you to keep this arrangement between us. Ma and Pa are wonderful parents, and I would hate to cause them distress. I will reveal details of my search to them when I know the time is right.

May the Lord comfort you as you grieve for your dear Mary.

Yours,

Hester

Satisfied with the wording of both letters, Hester folded the letter to her father inside the surgeon's and applied a large wax seal. She stowed the precious package inside her jacket for safekeeping. All she needed now was Giles Heale's address.

CHAPTER 20

HESTER PLACED Ma's delivery bag on the parlour table and packed it with a clean knife, sharpened scissors, a skein of thread, oils and clean linens.

'All done, Ma,' she said, when Ma emerged from the kitchen.

Ma peered inside the bag and pushed it aside. 'I think it's time,' she said, turning away from the table.

'Time for what?'

Ma fetched the basket filled with clothes awaiting repair. She placed it on the table and snatched one of Martha's night-smocks from the top. 'This,' she said, beaming at Hester.

Hester stared wide-eyed at a large leather bag nestling on a pile of shifts and shirts. 'Is that what I think it is?'

Ma lifted the bag and held it out to Hester. 'Your own delivery bag.'

'You think I'm ready?'

'I do.'

Hester's hand shook as she accepted the gift. 'I don't believe it.'

Ma laughed. 'Oh, Hester, you've attended countless births with me and shown yourself to be competent. You know what must be done, and you can always send for me if something untoward occurs and you need a little help.'

Hester placed her bag on the table and threw her arms around Ma's neck. Tears of joy spilled onto her cheeks. 'Thank you, Ma. I can't tell you what this means to me.'

Ma embraced her and patted her on the back. 'You already have a fine reputation to build upon, and I know you will make an excellent midwife.' Ma released her grip on Hester. 'Your independence begins today. Lydia Phillips is heavy with child. I expect her to deliver within the next week or two. Visit her, examine her and check that all is well. This will be her first baby, so take care to put her at ease so she trusts you when she travails.'

'I will.' Hester gave Ma a beaming smile. Lydia was married to Adam's older brother, and their house was near the forge. Visiting Lydia would give Hester an opportunity to see Adam. She was eager to confide in her friend and share her excitement about searching for her father – and she knew she could trust Adam to keep the revelation to himself.

'Oh, and you'll need this.' Ma pushed a large leather-bound book across the table. 'This is your very own journal for recording details of your patients.'

Hester ran her fingertips over the journal, relishing the feel of the soft grain of the leather. She opened the cover and flicked through the blank pages. The paper was of good quality, smooth to the touch and neatly trimmed at the edges.

'It's up to you how you use it,' Ma said. 'Chronological entries like mine, or a page per patient, like Pa's.'

Hester imagined returning home later, sitting at the table, turning to the first page and writing notes about Lydia Phillips. She would keep her notes similar to Ma's and include the date and location and describe the baby and the placenta. She would keep a column for special notes: what went well or any complications. Her notes would serve well as a reference for how she handled unusual or difficult situations. Then her thoughts drifted. Now, she had her own paper supply to use however she wished. If her father replied to her letter, it would be so easy for her to write to him again.

Hester hurried towards Lydia's house, full of anticipation. The April air was uncharacteristically warm, causing sweat to bead above her lip and across the back of her neck. In her mind, Hester rehearsed what she would say to Lydia. First, she would put her at ease, then she would explain what Lydia should expect, including a gentle warning that after the onset of labour, the contractions would grow closer together and increase in strength. She would explain to Lydia how to control her breathing and get her to practise so that she would understand Hester's commands when it mattered most. She would also explain to Lydia that there would be a brief delay between delivering the baby and delivering the placenta, but Hester decided not to tell her about how she would check that none of the placenta was missing. There was no need to instil her with fear that any fragments left behind might cause bleeding and fever or even a risk of death.

When Hester entered Lydia's house, she found Lydia composed and excited. Adam's mother had put her at ease by sharing accounts of her own four deliveries.

'You are well informed already,' Hester said, masking her disappointment that Lydia needed no explanations. 'Let me do a quick examination to check that all is well.'

Lydia glanced at Hester's stick. 'My bedchamber is upstairs.'

'Lead the way,' Hester said, relieved Lydia had a set of stairs and not a ladder like most of the older houses. And there was a handrail.

Hester used both hands to map out Lydia's baby. 'I can feel the baby's back,' she announced, 'and the baby's head is low in your pelvis.' She pulled Lydia's skirts down to cover her swollen belly. 'You don't have long to wait now,' she said, smiling. 'Perhaps a week or two.'

The sun was shining in a clear blue sky when Hester left the house. She grasped her stick and her bag in the same hand and adjusted the angle of her hat to shield her eyes from the glare.

'Hester!'

Adam was waving to her from the entrance to the forge. ''Tis a beautiful day,' Adam said, as Hester approached him. He smiled and took her bag from her so that she could remove her light woollen cloak.

''Tis a perfect day in so many ways,' Hester replied,

lingering by the open doors, preferring the gentle onshore breeze to the intolerable heat inside the forge.

'Is all well with my soon-to-be-born nephew or niece?'

'I believe so. Your sister-in-law shows none of the nerves that most first mothers endure.'

Adam wiped his sooty hands on a rag. 'She's a hardy one, that's for sure. Your mother didn't come with you today, then?'

'She's not my mother, Adam, as you well know.'

Adam's smile wavered. 'She is in all but blood.'

Hester shrugged. 'I can't deny she raised me well and taught me everything I know about midwifery. But even though I call her Ma, she will never be my mother. Not in the true sense of the word.' Hester lowered her voice. 'Adam, may I tell you something?'

Adam threw his soiled rag onto the floor inside the forge. 'Anything.'

'Promise you won't tell anyone?'

Adam pressed his palm to his chest. 'As God is my witness.'

Hester leaned towards him and lowered her voice to a whisper. 'I've written a letter to my father.'

Adam jerked away from her. The colour drained from his face. 'Why?'

Hester clenched her fingers until her nails dug into her palms. 'I thought you would share my excitement, Adam, because you are my friend.'

He shook his head. 'You should not have done that.'

'Why ever not?' Without giving Adam a chance to answer, Hester added. 'I need to know my father, Adam, if I'm to understand who I am.'

Adam reached into his jerkin. When he withdrew his hand, he had Shadow in his grasp. 'Please don't send it, Hester. I fear it won't end well. Your ma and pa had their reasons for keeping his existence to themselves.' He lowered Shadow to the ground and dropped a couple of walnuts. Shadow ignored them, preferring to explore an old, discarded sack.

'I thought it more normal for friends to share each other's joy.'

'I am your friend, Hester. That, you must never doubt.' Adam looked sideways at her. 'But I do not celebrate your revelation. I fear it will have consequences you do not expect.'

'Such as?'

'I don't know. But I know your ma and pa would only ever do what they thought was best for you. I fear for your happiness, that's all.'

'I intend to go to London,' Hester said, surprising herself with the announcement. It was something that had flitted through her mind but now felt like a decision.

A mother and child scurried along the road to a house with an open door. Hester could hear a cheerful exchange of greetings as they disappeared inside. 'I have a family in London. A father, and maybe half-brothers and sisters I've never met.'

Hester thought Adam turned a little pale. 'Maybe you have,' he said. 'But London's so far away.' Shadow lolloped across the ground and settled by Adam's feet. He held a scrap of torn cloth in his paws and chattered with little squeaks. Adam took the cloth from Shadow and curled his fingers tight around it. 'What if your father's situation is less idyllic than you think?'

'How bad can it be? I asked Ma and Pa about him, and they claim to know very little. Ma can't even remember where my parents lived. If their situation was so dreadful, she would not forget!'

Adam lowered his head. 'It's your right to find him, I suppose.'

'It is. The thought of seeing London gives me such a thrill! Imagine, Adam, ladies parading in elegant dresses, or riding in carriages pulled by horses with their coats brushed to a gleam.'

'London's not like that. Yes, there are wealthy ladies who go about as you describe. But most are not like that at all.'

Hester stiffened. 'How would you know?' The pleasure of being with Adam was dissipating fast.

Adam removed his thick protective apron and hung it on a hook fixed to the forge door. 'I was nine years of age when I left London,' he said, dabbing his forehead and neck with his shirt sleeve. 'I remember it well. So many streets are filthy, ankle-deep in mire. The houses are so close together that neighbours can reach out to each other from the upstairs windows and grasp each other's hands.' He nodded towards his brother's house, where Hester had visited Lydia. 'It's not like here. Most homes stand close together, and only wealthy people have gardens. Some houses might have a yard, while others must share, and whole families live in one small room instead of houses the size of ours. Crowds clog the streets from dawn until dusk, and the noise is persistent wherever you go. But worst of all, the air is foul and the city reeks.' Adam wrinkled his nose. 'I wouldn't dream of going back.'

'It can't all be as bad as that.' Hester struggled to imagine the scenes Adam had described. 'I know there's a theatre because I went there as a child. And there's a wide river with thousands of boats. It must be so colourful there!'

Adam took Hester's arm and turned her until she was facing the harbour. 'Look,' he said, pointing at the glistening sea in the distance. 'The sun strikes the water and creates millions of sparkling jewels. Are they not God's gifts to us for the toil that we do here? The Thames has no such jewels on its water. Instead, it is muddy, smelly, and churns up its filth where it passes beneath London Bridge.'

A sob rose in Hester's throat. She tried to swallow it away. 'I have to find my father.'

'Dearest Hester, it would break my heart to see you sail away from these shores. Please think for a while longer before committing to drastic plans.'

Adam had an earnest expression, the like of which Hester had never seen on his face before. Tears spilled onto her cheeks. 'It grieves me that you do not share my excitement. You are not the friend you declared yourself to be.'

'And yet I had hoped to be so much more.'

'My dearest friend?' Hester huffed. 'If that were true, you would want me to be happy and you would encourage me with my search.'

Adam bent towards the ground and picked up a jagged stone. He launched it towards the middle of the street. It landed with a thud and kicked up a cloud of dust. Shadow jerked upright, struggling to balance on his hind legs. His hair seemed to stand on end, and he flicked his tail back and forth before disappearing into the gloom of the forge. 'It's clear from your tone that no one will dissuade you from proceeding with your plan. I'm still sore from losing my father, so I'll try harder to understand.' Adam reached for Hester's hand. His hand was large but his touch was gentle, and his cool skin made Hester's burn where it brushed the backs of her fingers. 'If your heart will only mend in London, then London is where you must go.'

A wave of heat coursed through Hester from her arm to her neck and face. Adam had said what she wanted to hear, but there had been a touch of bitterness in his voice. She eased her hand away from Adam's. 'At the moment, it's impossible. I have no fare for a passage, and I don't know where my father lives.' Hester forced herself to smile. 'I thank you for your counsel and your words of support. Now I must bid you farewell and return to my home. Good day to you, Adam.'

Hester felt Adam watching her back as she walked away from the forge. Her walking stick clacked against rubble in the road, and her boots gathered a layer of dust. Her irritation at Adam's negativity dissipated as she drew nearer to her home. She would write her notes about Lydia and then return to her quest. She would do whatever it took to find Surgeon Heale's address.

CHAPTER 21

HESTER FINISHED WRITING up her notes about Lydia before joining Ma in the kitchen. 'Tell me about the surgeon,' she said as she started peeling an onion.

Ma was preparing a fish for supper. She cut the flesh away from the backbone and then ran her fingertip along the fillets to check for tiny bones. Sunlight streamed through the open window, catching small scales that clung to her hands and causing them to shimmer.

'Are you referring to Giles Heale?'

Hester's eyes watered as she chopped the pungent onion. She resisted the urge to dab her eyes, knowing it would make them sting. 'Yes. I have a vague recollection of his face, but it's no clearer than the outline of a sketch.'

Ma placed the fish fillets on a griddle and wiped her hands on her apron. 'He's a charming fellow. Intelligent and quick-witted. He loved debating medical practices with Pa, and they often talked late into the night. He's a kind man too. Mary often teased him for undercharging patients.'

Hester swept her pile of onion pieces into a hot pan. She added a generous handful of chopped parsley and a large knob of butter. The mixture sizzled and gave off a delicious aroma that made Hester's stomach gurgle. She felt a lightness in her chest as she reflected on Ma's words. Ma had referred to the surgeon's kindness, so it was probable he would help Hester locate her father.

'Did you live near Giles and Mary?' Somehow, Hester needed to ask the right question to get Ma to reveal the surgeon's address. She did not dare to rummage through Pa's private papers again.

Ma's expression turned wistful. 'We lived with them for several months. Mary was a darling. I arrived in London with very little to my name, and my clothes were inadequate for life in London. Mary shared her dresses with me until I bought more of my own.'

Hester was uninterested in Mary and her wardrobe. 'Does Giles still live in the same house?'

Ma furrowed her brow. 'I don't know. Not that it matters now. We're unlikely to see him again.'

'But Pa writes to him, so he must know where he lives.'

'I suppose he does.'

Samuel barrelled in from the garden looking pleased with himself. 'I did lots of digging and weeding, Ma. Pa said I did it well.'

'Have you fed the chickens today?' Hester asked, eager to send him outside again.

'This morning.'

'Then it's time you fed them again!'

'Must I? Pa said he'd play merels with me as a reward for working hard.'

Ma patted the top of Samuel's head. 'Do as your sister tells you and clean out the goat pen too. After that, you may play games with Pa.'

Hester waited for Samuel to leave the kitchen before throwing her next question at Ma.

'You were telling me about Giles and Mary.' Hester's hands shook a little as she used a spoon to lift onion pieces from the pan. She went to taste the onion, but her appetite evaporated and a sour taste rose into her mouth. She sniffed the onion instead and pressed the pieces to check they were soft. Returning them to the pan, she said, 'Where did you say they lived?'

Hot oil fizzed on the griddle. Ma cried out as oil spat and a small welt rose on the back of her hand. 'Somewhere near the heart of London.' She blew on her scalded skin. 'Just as well they did, too. Giles had several wealthy patients living in or close to his neighbourhood.'

'Did they have a grand house, the surgeon and his wife?'

Ma lifted the fish fillets from the griddle and laid them on a serving platter. 'Haven't we discussed them enough?' she replied irritably, studying a blister that had bubbled on the welt.

'I'm just interested.' Hester hoped Ma had not heard the desperate edge to her voice.

'Why so much interest in Giles? Aren't you more curious about where you lived?'

No, I am not. Hester suppressed her rising panic. She needed the name of the street where the surgeon had his house so she could coax Pa into confirming whether he still lived there. 'I'm trying to build a picture in my mind of what it was like for you and Pa when you moved from here to London. It must have been a very different life from the one you'd been living here.' Was that sufficient? Hester thought it might not be, so added, 'I've heard the odd tale about your time in Leyden, and plenty about the voyage that brought you to America. I'm eager to learn more about London.' Hester gave Ma an encouraging smile. 'If you're willing to tell me.'

'You want my life story?'

Hester laughed. 'Not all of it, Ma. I don't remember any of my time in London, and it's so difficult to imagine.'

Ma's expression turned wistful. 'There's no other place like it. I suppose I enjoyed my time in London, but I much prefer it here.'

Tension crept into Hester's muscles. She was so close to getting the information she needed. 'So, your life in London started with Giles and Mary Heale. Tell me how you knew where to find them.' Hester stirred the contents of her pan. The onion pieces were turning golden at the edges. She raised the pan higher above the fire to prevent them from charring and tasting bitter.

Ma poured them each a cupful of ale. 'We were exhausted by the time we reached London. The voyage was nowhere near as bad as the one we endured on the *Mayflower*, but it was long, and the sea was rough. I spent much of every night lying awake in our cabin.' She raised her cup to her lips and took a couple of sips. 'Did you know I was afraid of water when I was a girl?'

Hester shook her head. 'I didn't. It must have been a

great relief to stand on the bank of the River Thames after a rough voyage.'

'It was. It was an even greater relief to see Pa pay the ferryman and ask directions to Drury Lane. It meant our journey was almost over.'

A breath caught in Hester's throat. 'Jury Lane? Is that where Giles and Mary lived?'

'Drury, not Jury. Yes, they had a lovely home. The street appeared so elegant compared to the streets we left behind here. Every building had three storeys and glass in every window. None of the houses here had glass – we had wooden shutters and oiled paper.'

Hester thought about the older houses, built soon after the *Mayflower* arrived. Even now, none of them had glass in the windows and they were small and run down compared to where she lived with Ma and Pa.

Ma seemed wistful as she reminisced about her arrival in London. 'I remember standing outside Giles' house waiting for the door to open. There was a shiny brass plaque on the wall, proclaiming it the home of *Giles Heale, Surgeon.*'

Samuel flung open the kitchen door and hurried inside, dragging Pa by the hand. 'Now can we play?' he wheedled at Ma. 'I've done everything you asked.'

Hester was unbothered by the noisy intrusion this time. She had almost all the information she needed. A surgeon with a brass plaque on the wall of a house in Drury Lane. She watched Samuel dart into the parlour, eager to set the board for the game.

'You two look serious,' Pa said, looking concerned. 'Is something amiss?'

Ma smiled. 'Not at all. I was telling Hester about us living with Giles and Mary for a while in their house on Drury Lane.'

Hester seized her opportunity. 'Does Giles still live there, Pa?'

'Yes, he does, but for how much longer I cannot say. According to his letter, his brother Henry lives in St Giles-in-the-Fields. Now that Mary has passed away, he's considering moving nearer to Henry.'

So, time was of the essence! *Drury Lane. Drury Lane.* Hester repeated it many times in her mind to commit it to her memory. The next time she was alone at home, she would add the street name to the surgeon's letter and send it on its way.

An entire week dragged by and Hester still had not found an opportunity to add the surgeon's address to his letter. One warm spring morning, she woke before daybreak. The thin early light of dawn filtered through the shutters of the bedchamber window and painted a pale band across her pillow. She closed her eyes and strained her ears for sounds of movement elsewhere in the house, but all she could hear was a soft sigh from Martha followed by gentle breaths. Even the chickens were still silent in the yard.

Hester slipped out from under the coverlet and threw on her clothes. She pulled on her boots as fast as she could and quickly tied the laces before making her way down the stairs, taking care to avoid squeaky floorboards.

Excitement surged through Hester as she approached Pa's writing desk to take a quill and ink. She opened the drawer and rolled her eyes when she discovered all his quills were blunt. She eased open another drawer and rummaged around until she found a knife. As she withdrew it, she caught Pa's seal in her sleeve, and it fell to the floor with a clatter. Hester froze. Her pulse pounded so loud in her ears it would not have surprised her if the neighbours could hear it. She waited for what felt like several long minutes. Satisfied that she would not be disturbed, she sat on Pa's chair. She wiped her sweating palms on her skirt before sharpening the quill, and then, in her neatest hand, she wrote the surgeon's address.

Surgeon Giles Heale
Drury Lane
London.

She stared at the words on the paper and prayed that they sufficed to locate one man among the thousands living in the city.

Voices drifted down the stairs. Ma and Pa were awake. Hester blew across the words to make sure the ink had dried. She tucked the letter into the pocket tied at her waist, then grabbed her stick and hurried to the kitchen. She built up the fire ready to cook breakfast, and set the table with wooden plates, cups and a pitcher of ale. The cockerel crowed in the yard as Pa's footsteps thundered down the stairs. Hester greeted him with a beaming smile and invited him to sit. They discussed his busy day ahead and the patients he would visit. She fried him a slice of salted bacon with two griddled eggs, then sat with him while he ate, unable to eat herself.

Hester sat with her palm resting on her pocket. The package of letters was ready to travel all the way to England. All she needed now was a ship.

CHAPTER 22

THE END of April was approaching and Lydia had not yet delivered her baby. Hester decided to pay her a visit to check that all was well, and afterwards she would visit Adam to seek his advice about sending her letter package to England.

A heavy shower had washed the dust from the air, and the temperature was pleasant. Birds sang high in the trees, and gardens were awash with colour. Hester stopped to pluck a violet and held it to her nose, relishing the sweet scent from the delicate purple flower. She dropped the bloom into the hedgerow and continued with her walk, but as she approached Lydia's house a tension built in her shoulders and across the back of her neck. She murmured a quick prayer, asking for God's guidance. 'Let this delivery go smoothly, Lord, especially as it's my first without Ma.'

Lydia appeared more apprehensive than she had been during Hester's previous visit. She held both hands pressed to her lower back and moved about her bedchamber with slow lumbering steps. Wincing and groaning, Lydia lay down on her bed so that Hester could examine her and check the position of her unborn baby.

'Have you felt the babe move today?' Hester asked, trying to sound calm.

Lydia grimaced as she thought. 'I think so,' she replied. 'Perhaps earlier this morning?'

Hester pressed harder on Lydia's taut skin and detected a flutter of movement. Relieved the baby was still alive, she eased Lydia up to a sitting position. 'Is your back still aching?'

'It comes and goes.' Lydia pursed her lips and let out a long breath.

'Was that the pain again?'

Lydia nodded. 'It's getting worse.'

Hester gave her a reassuring smile. 'I have good news, Lydia. You are in the early stages of labour. I have an errand to run, but it won't take too long. I'll be back within an hour or two, and then I won't leave you again until after your child is born.'

As Hester went to step away, Lydia grasped her arm. 'I'm frightened, Hester.'

Hester covered Lydia's hand with hers. 'When a mother labours for the first time, it's always a little daunting. Try not to worry. I'll use my soothing oils and do everything I can to keep you comfortable.' Hester paused. Ma often used those very words when she attended first-time mothers. Hester added, 'You're going to be a mother, Lydia. You are blessed.'

Lydia's bottom lip quivered. 'That's what worries me. What if I'm no good at it?'

'You will be.' Hester tried to sound reassuring but did not feel she had the right to assert such a thing. 'You can only do your best,' she said. 'That's what matters most. I'm going to leave you now, but I'll be back before you know it. Stay on your feet and keep moving. It will help ease your back.'

Lydia took a slow deep breath. 'My mother-in-law will be here soon. She'll keep me calm.'

'What about your own mother?' It occurred to Hester that Lydia had made no mention of her.

Lydia grasped the back of a chair. She leaned forward and pursed her lips and seemed to hold her breath. At last, she said, 'My mother died when I was a girl, but Adam's mother treats me as one of her own.'

Hester felt her jaw tighten. 'I'll be quick,' she said, retrieving her bag. She needed to speak to Adam.

The heat from the forge engulfed Hester several steps before she reached the large open door. The warm air carried the smells of hot metal, smoke and toil. She found Adam hard at work inside and watched him hammer a piece of glowing metal into the shape of a horseshoe. He plunged the metal into a bucket of water, making it hiss and steam. Then he withdrew the horseshoe and placed it on a rack to cool. He greeted Hester with a wave, but his cheery smile was missing. Hester walked across the forge towards him. She plucked a linen square from her sleeve and offered it to Adam.

Adam wiped his hands on his thick leather apron before accepting the clean linen square. 'I think you should end the search for your father.'

'Why?'

'I believe you're making a mistake.' Adam blotted his brow. 'Your ma and pa took you in and raised you, believing it to be for the best. Now you're as good as casting them aside.'

'No, I'm not! I'm still fond of them both, but my feelings have shifted a little because of what they did.' Hester felt a tightening in the pit of her stomach. She was certain Adam's friendship was cooling. 'Please understand, Adam, my yearning to meet my father grows stronger every day. I cannot sleep because of the need to find him. Until I do, I will never feel whole again.' Hester studied Adam's face, hoping to find a glimmer of empathy or encouragement. She found neither. 'I'm sad that you try to dissuade me. I thought you understood.'

Adam met her gaze for a few long seconds. 'What if your father is not a good man? The way you favour him after all these years must be distressing for your Ma and Pa.' He held out the sweat-soaked linen.

'Keep it,' Hester said. 'You might need it again.'

Adam reached for a heavy hammer and pounded another piece of hot metal. Once he had finished shaping the end, he threw the hammer onto the earthen floor. 'Do you deny that your Ma and Pa love you as their own?'

Hester frowned at the divot left by the hammer. 'No.' She bent to retrieve the hammer and struggled under its weight. She placed it on the workbench, beyond Adam's reach. 'When my father fled after I was born, his emotions must have been in turmoil. He had lost his wife! Few men would embrace the idea of raising a child alone.' She turned to look at Adam. 'My father's life will be different now, and he might welcome his long-lost daughter. I think of him every day, but I can't picture his face. I must find him, Adam, for my own sake and perhaps for his.'

'I wish I could dissuade you. You're making a mistake.' He pushed past her to retrieve his hammer and pounded the metal rod again. Hester sensed he did not want her to stay, but she needed to ask him a question.

'Adam?'

Adam continued pounding the metal as if he had not heard her. Tiny sparks flew into the air as metal struck against metal.

'Adam!' The urgency in her voice caused Adam to stop and look up. 'I have never sent a letter before. Who do I ask to take it to London?'

'Have you written it?'

Hester placed her hand over her pocket and nodded.

A nerve twitched at Adam's right temple. 'There's a ship lying at anchor in the harbour. It will set sail for London soon. I'll find a member of the crew willing to take it for you.'

'Thank you. Your help means so much to me.'

Adam snorted. 'I hope you don't come to regret it.'

Hester turned to walk away, but Adam called out to her. 'You'll have to pay the fellow in coins, Hester, so have a purse of money ready.'

Hester bid Adam a cool farewell and hurried home as

fast as her limp would allow. She topped up her bottle of soothing oil and packed her bag with everything she would need to have ready for Lydia's labour. Then she climbed the stairs to her bedchamber and retrieved the purse Widow Morton had given her for attending to her ulcer. She prayed it held sufficient coins to pay for her letters to travel to England and reach the surgeon's door.

CHAPTER 23

THE BEDCHAMBER WAS STIFLING. Hester longed to open a window and take gulping breaths of cool night air. She was also hungry and thirsty, and after the long hours spent with Lydia, her patience was wearing thin. Adam's mother had joined them hours ago, and her presence seemed to fill the room. She had an aroma of stale fried fish that made Hester's stomach turn. Hester found her irritating as she fussed around Lydia, dabbing her forehead with a damp cloth and praising Lydia's feeble attempts whenever Hester instructed her to push. Hester considered ejecting her from the room but fought back her frustration and concentrated on the task at hand. At last, Lydia gave her final push, and the baby slithered into the world.

'You have a son, Lydia,' Hester announced, wiping blood and vernix from his skin. She checked he had all his fingers and toes and then turned him over on her lap to check the shape of his spine. 'A handsome little fellow he is too.' She stroked the delicate skin of his wrinkled little face and traced the outline of his rosebud mouth. This was her first delivery without Ma, and it had proceeded without a hitch. As she wrapped the baby in a small clean sheet, he gave a lusty cry, opening his mouth wide enough to reveal his tongue was tied. Hester rocked him back and forth to soothe him and instructed Mistress Phillips to make Lydia comfortable so that she could hold her baby boy. As soon as Mistress Phillips took her eye off her grandson, Hester withdrew her scissors from her delivery bag. The scissors felt heavy in her hand as she checked they were sharp while steeling herself to cut the band that restricted the baby's tongue. She had watched Ma do it many a time, and it only took a second. Holding her breath, she made the snip and watched a small trickle of blood emerge. Hester pressed beneath the baby's tongue with a corner of the sheet, and by the time Lydia was ready to hold her son, the bleeding had stopped.

Mistress Phillips held out her arms to take the baby from Hester, but Hester pretended not to see her and said, 'Here he is, Lydia. Your precious little boy.'

Lydia beamed as she reached for her baby. 'My Benjamin,' she said, stroking his brow. 'Your father will be so thrilled to meet you when he arrives home.'

Hester returned to the foot of the bed to deliver the afterbirth, enjoying Lydias's coos and exclamations of joy. Satisfied that the placenta was complete and Lydia was recovering well from her labour, Hester tidied around her and returned her knife, scissors and soothing oil to her delivery bag.

The baby became agitated and screwed up his face. He

held his breath for a few seconds and then let out an angry wail.

'Your son is hungry,' Hester said. 'Shall I show you how to put him to your breast?'

Lydia looked at Mistress Phillips. 'Mother?'

Mistress Phillips nodded. 'I can do that,' she said to Hester. 'But thank you.'

'In that case, I'll leave you be.' Hester slipped her arm through the handles of her delivery bag and retrieved her walking stick from where she had left it propped by the bedchamber door. She turned to face Mistress Phillips. 'Forgive me, but there is the small matter of payment.'

'Of course!' Mistress Phillips looked a little discomfited and made no move to fetch a purse or a coffer. 'I'm afraid I have no money to give you, Hester, but you must visit Adam at the forge and request whatever items you desire. Skillets, pans, knives and cauldrons. Please request them all!'

Hester tried to find an appropriate response but could think of none. It was not unusual for women to pay in kind, but it was coins Hester desired.

'Come now, Hester. Don't be shy. One day, you'll have a home of your own, and you'll be glad of all those items.'

Hester wondered if spinsters ever lived alone. She could not think of one in the colony. 'I would welcome a new pair of scissors,' she said at last. 'Mine have worn thin from sharpening.'

'Scissors it is, then. But you must choose several other items as well.'

'I will. Thank you.' Hester cast a last glance in Lydia's direction. Lydia had the flushed look of love Hester had seen on new mothers before, and the baby was making soft gulping sounds as he suckled at her breast. She wondered what it felt like to hold a baby so close but then dismissed her musings and thought about her letters instead. Adam had warned her she would need to pay for the little package to sail to England. A promise of iron-mongery was no good for that. Her pocket knocked against her as she walked, causing the coins inside to jangle. Her chest tightened as she wondered what to do if they proved to be insufficient.

Hester was relieved to find Adam still at the forge but thought he might be about to leave because he had allowed the fire to burn low. He grew disgruntled with her arrival, and more distant than before. Hester apolo-gised for her intrusion and relayed the instruction his mother had given about requesting payment in kind.

'Are you sure that's all you want?' Adam said, with a frosty edge to his voice. 'Scissors, a small knife and a few pins for your hair? There's nothing else you would like?'

'There's no point in my requesting heavy pots and cauldrons,' Hester said. 'Not while there's a chance I might sail to England.'

Adam pressed his fist to his forehead. 'This nonsense again! Why, Hester? Why would you go to England? You know nothing about the country apart from what other people have told you.'

'Isn't that enough? You knew nothing about life in America until your parents brought you here.' Hester tightened her grasp of her walking stick and took a steadying breath. 'My father might want me to live with him there.'

'God's bones! Must you be so pig-headed?'

Hester gasped. 'Adam!'

'How can you contemplate living with a man you have never met! It's not only foolish. It's dangerous.' Adam's top lip twitched as if resisting saying more. Eventually, he said, 'Please, Hester, I beg you to drop this pursuit of such madness.'

'Why, Adam? What could be more important than being with my true family?'

Adam's reply came loud and sharp. 'I hoped I was!'

Hester gasped and raised her hand to her mouth. 'Oh! I…'

Adam spun away from her and ran his fingers through his hair. His hands seemed to shake a little. Hester watched him pace the forge, muttering to himself. He passed by a shelf stacked with horseshoes and punched a pile with his fist. They fell off the shelf and struck the floor with a series of loud metal clangs. Hester shifted her weight onto her normal foot, wishing Adam would calm down.

'I don't know how to tell you this, Hester,' Adam said, coming to a halt in front of her. 'I thought you already knew.' He took her walking stick from her and laid it across his workbench. Taking both of her hands in his, he said, 'My feelings for you run deeper than friendship. With all my heart, I love you.'

Hester jerked her hands away as if scalded by his touch. She could not deny having feelings for Adam but she refused to let them develop into something deeper. She did not believe herself worthy of his love. And she had a letter in her pocket that had a chance of reaching her father. 'That's not love you feel for me, Adam. It's compassion born of our friendship.'

Adam shook his head and tried to interrupt, but Hester silenced him with a glare. 'Love is not for someone like me. It's more suited to girls like Martha.' She reached for her walking stick and gripped it so hard that her knuckles paled. 'No man can love me the way I am, not while I need this.' She tapped her stick on the hard floor, leaving a shallow divot. 'I don't even know who I am.'

A long silence hung between them. A piece of wood shifted in the forge fire and sent up a shower of sparks.

'Hester,' Adam said, lowering his voice. 'What if your father is dead?'

Hester rubbed the handle of her walking stick with the pad of her thumb. 'Then I'll never be certain of who I am, and I'll always feel adrift.'

'I'd better get back to work,' Adam said, his voice sounding thick with sadness. 'I'll have your scissors, knife and pins ready for you within a day or two.'

'Thank you.' Hester walked towards the door, her stick tapping hard against the beaten earth floor. She stopped abruptly in the doorway and turned. 'You said you would find someone to take my letter to London. Did you?'

'Yes.' Hester caught a flat look in Adam's eyes. 'There's a fellow who goes by the name of Moses,' he said. 'He's in charge of loading the ship. They'll sail as soon its loaded, so you don't have a lot of time. You'll spot him easily enough. He's the tallest fellow I've ever seen.' Adam gestured to a long shelf buckling under the weight of skillets, trivets, fire irons and bolts. 'I could give you anything you want, Hester.' His voice cracked when he added, 'But you have made it very plain I cannot give you enough.'

Hester's throat tightened. She turned and walked out of the forge.

Hester hurried to the harbour hoping to find Moses before twilight turned to night. She spotted a giant of a man with straw-coloured hair towering above his fellow sailors as they loaded pelts onto a tender. After launching the last bundle onto the rowing boat, Moses yelled at a crewman to jump aboard and made as if to board himself.

'Moses! Moses, wait!' Hester hobbled across the beach, her boots crunching across sand and shingle.

'What do you want?' The sailor towered above Hester, casting her in shadow. He had a thickset body and a large scar running from the top of his wind-ravaged left cheek all the way to the corner of his lips.

Hester had to force herself to look up at his face. 'Adam Phillips said you might help me.'

'Did he now? Ship leaves in a few minutes, so you'd better tell me what you want.' He looked Hester up and down and wrinkled his nose.

'He said you would deliver a letter for me. I need it to go to London.'

'Aye, I can do that for you.' He held out his hand and clicked his fingers. 'Hand it over.'

Hester tucked her walking stick under her arm and

withdrew the precious letter package from her pocket. 'I need it to go to an address in Drury Lane. Is that something you can do?'

The sailor snorted and spat out a gobbet of phlegm. Hester heard it land with a splat on the shingle near her boot. She shuddered. Never had she had dealings with someone so uncouth.

'I can do it for a price.'

'I can pay you a shilling.' Hester untied the pocket from her waist and reached in for the purse.

The sailor guffawed. 'A shilling? I'll have to travel across London to get to Drury Lane. For that, I'll need a carriage.'

Hester's mouth turned dry. She found it hard to swallow. 'A carriage?' Only the wealthiest merchants in Boston travelled in a carriage. She dropped the purse back into her pocket. 'I don't have enough money for that. I'm sorry to have troubled you.'

As she turned to leave the beach, the sailor grabbed her arm. Hester's whole body tensed.

'I'll do it for three shillings,' he said, releasing her to wipe his nose on his shirtsleeve.

A sharp pain shot from Hester's foot to her knee. She quickly returned her stick to her hand and used it to take her weight. 'How do I know you'll take my letter all the way to Drury Lane?'

The sailor smirked. 'You don't. Our transaction requires trust. I can take a horse without a carriage, but three shillings is my price.'

Hester pulled out the small purse again and loosened the lace tie. She tipped the coins onto the sailor's hand. 'Two shillings,' she said, disheartened. 'That's all I have.'

'Hester!'

Hester froze at the sound of Pa's voice.

The sailor curled his fingers over the coins. 'Two shillings will suffice.' He snatched the letter from Hester's hand and strode towards the tender.

'Hester! Was that man bothering you?'

'No, Pa! We were just...' Hester's voice faded away. She had no desire to discuss with Pa her business with the sailor. She noticed Pa had a florid face, and he was panting for breath. 'Pa, are you sickening for something?'

'No, Hester. You were gone for so long. We were worried about you. I went to the Phillips' home to check all was well, and Adam said you had mentioned coming to the harbour. I could not imagine what would bring you here, so I came as fast as I could.'

Dear Adam, Hester thought, *thank you for keeping my secret.*

'Was that sailor harassing you?'

'No, Pa. We were talking. Nothing more.'

Pa narrowed his eyes. 'Did I see you give him money?'

Hester clamped her lips together, trying to think of a suitable response. But the sailor was far less discreet than Adam and brandished her letter package in the air.

'Don't worry, miss,' he yelled. 'I'll deliver this for you.'

Hester's pulse quickened and thundered in her ears.

'What... have... you... done?'

Hester forced herself to look at Pa. His face was taut with anger. She thrust out her chin and spoke with a confidence that surprised even herself. 'You kept my father's existence a secret for longer than you should have done. Now I wish to find the man who gave me his blood and give him the chance to learn about the daughter he hasn't seen for almost eighteen years.'

Pa clenched his fist and pressed it to his forehead, knocking it against his brow. Hester felt compelled to look away and glanced towards the rowing boat. Her gaze landed on Moses. He gave her a mischievous grin.

'That letter is on its way to Giles Heale,' Hester said. 'It encloses another letter.' She turned back to look at Pa. 'Now I must wait for a reply and pray it brings word from my father.'

A strange expression settled on Pa's face. His eyes looked cold, and he appeared to flinch. *Is it frustration?* Hester wondered. *Is it fear?* A shiver passed through her. *No, that's not fear. It's disgust.*

'We tried so hard to protect you, Hester,' Pa said in an unsteady voice.

'From what?' she replied tartly, watching the rowing boat cut through the water and approach the ship.

Pa started backing away. 'My dear, you do not know what you have done. I can only pray that letter never reaches its destination.' He turned his back towards Hester and took a few long strides.

'If it doesn't,' Hester shouted, 'I'll only write again!'

CHAPTER 24

THE LOFT WAS sultry with trapped summer air, even though the window shutters were wide open. There was no whiff of a gentle breeze nor a whisper of a draught. Bright sunlight streamed through the glass and struck surfaces thick with dust. Hester washed the dust away with large squares of cloth and she hung up small posies of fresh lavender to sweeten the musty air. Next, she swept up the dirt from the floorboards while Ma sorted through old clothes. The morning seemed to drag by, not helped by Ma's reluctance to talk.

'Ma, I'm sorry to have caused you so much distress. Please tell me why my writing to my father has hurt you so much?'

Ma returned a pile of old kirtles to a large sturdy chest and lowered the lid. The shrill squeak of old hinges made Hester wince.

'Hester, there are some things that are best left unsaid.' Ma used her palms to wipe sweat from her brow and then used the chest as a seat. 'If your father replies to your letter, he can explain things to you better than I ever could.' She pressed her hands together and raised her fingers to her lips. Hester wondered if she was praying or holding back tears. 'I hoped this situation would never arise. You have been our daughter since the day you were born, and we have always treated you as an equal to the children of our blood. We have given you a good life in a comfortable home. It grieves me that that isn't enough.'

Hester perched beside Ma and rested her hands on her lap. The heat from her palms burned on her thighs despite the layers of her skirts. 'I never intended to hurt you, Ma.'

'You have family and friends who love you,' Ma said, her voice breaking as she spoke.

'I know. I wish I could change the way I feel and accept things as they are. But I can't.' Hester stared through the window at an expanse of blue sky. Tiny silhouettes of herring gulls moved in the distance, gliding through the air, wheeling in large circles. 'Sometimes I feel like I'm a small bird flying beneath a vast sky. There are other birds up there with me, but they are fast and colourful while I am slow and dull.' Hester lowered her voice. 'I've ended up in the wrong flock, but the other birds don't mind.'

A thick cobweb had stuck to Ma's skirt. She brushed it away. 'Is it because of your foot?'

Hester raised her left leg and glared at her boot. 'No, I don't think it's that, although it marks me out as different from everyone else.' Hester allowed her foot to drop so the heel of her boot kicked dust up from the floor. She tapped her breastbone. 'It's something in here. It started building long before I learned about my birth. Then, when you told me what happened to my mother, the feeling made sense. The only way I can make it right is to find my father and talk to him. I need to know that he regrets running away from me, and I want him to tell me every little detail about my real mother.'

Ma clenched both of her hands, draining the colour from her knuckles. Hester worried she might draw blood from her palms if she clenched them any harder.

'Hester, what if your father is not the man you hope he will be?'

'Do you expect that to be the case?'

Ma shook her head. 'That's a question I cannot answer. I saw him for only an hour or two, many years ago. My guess is as good as yours as to the man he is now.'

'Precisely, Ma! People can change with their situation. He might have made a good life for himself and wish I were there to share it.'

Ma tutted. 'If your father responds to your letter, I will give him the benefit of the doubt. But if you hear nothing, you must accept your loss and embrace the life you have.'

'I'll try.' Hester leaned against Ma, finding comfort from her softened tone and her familiar scent of rose.

'I understand a little of what you're going through,' Ma said. 'Someone abandoned me too, but in a different manner.'

'I didn't know that. You haven't mentioned it before.'

Ma took a deep breath and released it through narrowed lips. 'My father died when I was sixteen years old, and my mother sent me into service. Soon after that, she remarried.' Ma paused for what seemed like an age. Hester allowed the silence to linger, sensing that Ma's memory was painful. 'I saw my mother before coming here on the *Mayflower*,' Ma said at last. 'We didn't have long together. She was expecting another child, and there was no place for me in her new husband's home. One of her parting gifts to me was the mirror you love so much. I tried to find her a few years later when Pa and I went to Leyden, but she and her husband had moved away and had told no one where they were going.' Ma stood and crossed the loft to open a small wooden chest. She rummaged inside and drew out something small wrapped in thin wool cloth. 'My mother gave me this, too.' Ma peeled back the covering to reveal a lace collar. The fabric had yellowed and thinned with age but had kept an air of elegance. 'I wore this collar the day I married Pa. I had hoped you might wear it on your wedding day, but the law has put paid to that!'

Hester limped across the creaking floorboards to inspect the collar. 'It's lovely.' She had forgotten the beauty a piece of lace could hold and cursed the strict Puritan laws that banned possession of such elegant items. She ran her finger over the lace edging and traced the petals of tiny flowers. Her throat constricted and her stomach hardened as she felt a flash of anger. Ma had something that she treasured, given to her by her mother, while Hester had nothing from hers. She tried to conceal her anger as she drew her hand away.

Ma held the collar to her lips and kissed the lace before returning it to its wrapping. 'May God forgive me for admiring this beautiful adornment.' Her tone turned bitter. ''Tis a strict world we live in now, Hester. While the merchants indulge their sin of greed and make fortunes from trading their wares, we must live a pure and godly life and take joy from all that is plain.' She returned the collar to the chest and slammed the lid. 'We have finished our work up here for the day. Let us take a cooling cup of ale outdoors and enjoy a few minutes in the shade.'

Hester waited for Ma to descend from the loft first while taking a moment to calm her rage. She tried to take comfort from sharing their losses, believing Ma understood how she felt. Hester even dared to hope that Ma would share her joy if the day ever arrived when she received her father's reply.

CHAPTER 25

AUGUST ARRIVED with a welcome balance of sunshine and rain. The farms promised bountiful crops and the sea yielded a generous supply of fish. Hester worked alongside Ma and Martha, salting cod for the winter months. She pickled onions, dried herbs and preserved apples and berries. Ma had been in better spirits since their conversation in the loft, and they worked together in easy companionship while Martha sang as she worked.

One balmy day in the middle of the month, Samuel barrelled into the still room. His cheeks were hot with colour and he was gasping for breath. 'There's a letter for Hester,' he said, brandishing a folded piece of paper and studying her reaction with interest.

Hester's hand trembled as she took the letter from Samuel. Someone had written her name in a neat script. She hoped it was her father's writing, but Ma took one look at the letter and said, 'That will be from Giles.'

Hester assessed the thickness of the folded paper. It was too thin to hold another note inside.

'Read it to us,' Samuel pleaded. 'Tell us what it says!'

The walls of the still room seemed to close in as Hester tucked the letter into a fold of her apron. 'I'd rather not,' she snapped in reply.

'Why don't you take it into the yard?' Martha suggested. 'You must be eager to know what it says.'

'That's a good idea,' Ma said. 'Take as long as you need to read it.'

Ma had a pained expression, although Hester could tell she was trying to hide it. Just because the letter was thin, it did not mean the surgeon had not found her father. There was still a chance her father would write too. Perhaps he just needed time.

Hester nodded at Ma and retrieved her walking stick from a hook on the back of the door. She crossed the yard and stood in the shade, staring towards the vegetable garden. What if the surgeon had not found her father? What would she do then? Hester pulled the letter from the fold of her apron and held it with a trembling hand. *Hester Trelawney*, it said in clear script. A hen waddled over to her and cocked her head, as if expecting Hester to offer her grain. Hester shooed the hen away and studied the handwriting again. The 'H' of her first name had flamboyant loops and swirls while the remaining letters appeared rather plain. Did it suggest there was good news inside? It was impossible to tell. Hester took a few deep breaths before she cracked the seal. Tiny red wax fragments fluttered towards her apron, clinging like tiny specks of blood. Her palms turned clammy as she opened the folds, taking care not to tear the paper.

Surgeon Giles Heale
Church Street
St-Giles-in-the-Fields
London

July 1645

My dear Hester,

First, my gratitude for your kind condolences. I am still struggling to come to terms with a life without my beloved Mary. However, one must move on, and she would not have wanted me to wallow in misery. I have therefore sold our house in Drury Lane and purchased a new house on the street where my brother lives. Matthew, his son, is eager to pursue a career as a surgeon and has almost finished his apprenticeship. We spend contented evenings discussing interesting cases and our preferred methods of treatment.

Enough of that! You must be eager to learn what happened to the letter you asked me to deliver to your father. I remembered the address of where you were born and had my servant boy pay it a visit. With regret, I must tell you that your father had long since moved away, and the new tenants denied knowing where he went. But, Hester, do not despair. Twisselton is an uncommon name, and I will track him down. I have made a list of likely establishments I believe he might frequent, and I have many contacts in London who will spread the word that I wish to see him. If your father is still living in this city, I will ensure he receives your letter.

Please pass on my fondest wishes to your ma and pa and tell them I will write to them when I am settled here.

May God bless you and keep you safe.

Giles Heale

A tear spilled onto the letter. Hester watched it spread through the paper, causing the ink to run and fade. It had landed on the word "father" and erased all the letters. She feared it might be an omen, a sign her father was dead. She refolded the paper and tucked the letter into her bodice, pressing it close to her heart. The surgeon had told her not to give up hope, and she would do as he said.

CHAPTER 26

THE MONTHS PASSED. The trees changed colour. Leaves swirled in the autumn winds. A few ships came and went, but Hester received no word from her father. One day, someone knocked at the door and set Hester's heartbeat racing. They weren't expecting anyone to call – no friends, neighbours or patients. Hester rushed to open the door and found Adam standing on the threshold. He was grasping his hat in both hands, and the wind was ruffling his hair.

'Will you walk with me?' he asked.

A cold draught whipped around Hester's legs, causing her to shiver. She looked over her shoulder at Ma.

'Go,' Ma said, flicking her hand. 'Bring Samuel when you come home. He's had a long day of learning at the Samsons' house and no doubt has tested Henry's patience.'

Hester pulled her fur-lined cloak from a peg by the door. The muted grey hue of the sky threatened early winter snow. 'In that case, I will walk with you, Master Adam Phillips.'

Adam reacted with a smile. Hester could not help but smile back.

Ma handed Hester her stick. 'Take care out there,' she said. 'There's an ill wind brewing.'

Hester eased her fingers into her soft leather gloves and grasped her walking stick. She wiggled her toes inside her stockings, grateful for the strips of rabbit pelt that added warmth to her boots. Adam offered her his arm, and she graciously accepted. They strolled along deserted streets and headed towards the harbour until they came across a tree uprooted by a recent storm. They used the trunk as a seat and sat staring at the roiling sea.

'I pity the poor devils sailing on that,' Adam said. 'If the water is choppy here, imagine how rough it is further out.'

Hester shifted position on the tree trunk until she was facing Adam. 'I feared our friendship had cooled in recent months. I've seen so little of you since the spring.'

'You misinterpreted my words and emotions, Hester. My feelings for you remain unchanged.'

'But when I've had cause to visit the forge, you didn't seem to want me there.'

Adam stared back out to sea. He cleared his throat, and Hester thought he was about to speak but then seemed to change his mind.

'Why, Adam? We have always enjoyed an easy friendship, but my search for my father has changed that. It's as if you don't want me to succeed.'

'I won't deny that I hoped you would give it up.'

Hester remained silent and waited for him to explain. She closed her eyes and breathed through her nose, inhaling Adam's musky, herbal scent.

'Do you remember that time I told you I loved you?'

Hester opened her eyes and chuckled. 'Yes, I do. We have been friends for many years, Adam. I have a special fondness for you too.'

'My feelings run much deeper than that. I know you so well, Hester. How you think, your opinions, your skills, your hopes and dreams. There is nothing I would change about you – except one thing.'

'And that is?'

'Your talk of travelling to England.'

'If I don't hear from my father, I'll have no reason to go. But if I do receive word from him, my dream will have come true.'

A heavy silence settled between them. A gust of wind whipped up a pile of dead leaves and twigs, sending them swirling along the ground. Waves crashed against the beach, roaring and hissing as they dragged sand and shingle in their wake.

'Would you come back to Plimoth?' Adam asked.

Hester thought of her recurring daydream of a joyful reunion with her father. She imagined her father showing her his home. It might not be a grand affair, but she would have a bed cloaked in clean sheets and maybe a chamber of her own. She imagined sitting at a table with her father's new wife and a half-sibling or two, swapping tales about their pasts and the future they would share. It was a cosy scene, loaded with possibilities. 'Truth be told, Adam, I don't think I would.' She pouted. 'I won't be going anywhere soon. I'll have to earn enough money to pay for my passage before I can leave these shores.'

Adam slapped his hands against the tree trunk, startling Hester.

'Why so angry, Adam?'

'I'm not angry,' he replied through almost clenched teeth. He rose to his feet and took a few steps before striding back and coming to a halt in front of her. He took a deep breath and said, 'Hester, I wish to marry you.'

Hester was taken aback and fumbled for something to say. 'Adam Phillips, have you taken leave of your senses?' She rose from the trunk and faced him. 'As much as I'm flattered by your proposal, I cannot become your wife.' She brandished the walking stick he had made. 'The warmth of our friendship has clouded your judgement. It's compassion you feel for me. What would your friends say if we were to marry? "Look at the handsome farrier," they'd cry. "There must be something wrong with him if needs a cripple for his wife."'

'No, Hester,' Adam said. 'My feelings for you are genuine.'

Hester adjusted her cloak while trying to compose her thoughts. Adam was someone she cared about – nay, someone she loved. But she had a greater yearning than to become Adam's wife. She was on an important quest and could let nothing get in her way. When she found her father, she would reevaluate her situation. By then she would know exactly who she was and would no longer feel incomplete.

Adam appeared deflated. 'I thought you harboured affection for me.'

'Of course I do.' Hester reached for his arm. 'You are and always will be very dear to me. Come,' she said, eager to change the subject, 'we must collect Samuel before Master Samson reaches his wits' end. Ma and Pa hope he'll take on Samuel as his apprentice. Then they will see more of him than if he moves to Boston.'

They walked together in silence, both deep in thought. Hester soon forgot about Adam's proposal as she imagined a different life abroad. In a city as busy as London, people might not notice her flaws. She would become a sought-after midwife and earn a decent wage. Her father would be so proud of her and brag about her skills. She would be a doting big sister and, later, a cherished aunt. She gazed back towards the ocean and scanned the jagged waves. Releasing Adam's arm, she cried, 'Adam! There's a ship!'

Adam raised his hand to his brow and squinted into the distance. 'Indeed, there is.'

'It might come bearing a letter from my father.'

Adam unhooked his arm from Hester's and turned his back towards the sea. 'Hester, I understand the importance to you of finding your father, but I wish it were not so. I cannot help but fear for you.'

'Oh, Adam, what harm could befall me? I'll have a new family that will welcome me into their home.'

'You don't know that.'

'Why wouldn't they?'

Adam hung his head. 'As God is my witness, I hope you find the contentment you seek.'

Hester beamed at Adam. 'I knew you would understand how I feel, and that means everything to me.'

CHAPTER 27

THERE WAS no letter for Hester.

The days grew shorter. The nights grew darker. Strong winds battered the house. The windows rattled in their casements, and neighbours helped one another repair sections of thatch on their roofs.

One stormy evening, Hester arrived home from delivering a baby to find the parlour fire had burned out. As she lay kindling ready to relight it, Martha bustled into the room.

'Leave that, Hester. Ma let it go out because the wind kept catching the chimney and blowing smoke into the room.'

Hester took a deep breath through her nose. 'The air doesn't reek of smoke.'

Ma called out from the kitchen. 'Is that Hester?'

'Yes, Ma,' Martha shouted in reply. 'We're coming.' To Hester she said, 'We've had no problems with a smoking fire in the kitchen, so we're keeping ourselves warm in there.' She extended her arm and gestured for Hester to lead the way.

Hester opened the door to find Ma, Pa and Samuel standing by the kitchen table. Three large wax candles burned at its centre, surrounded by an array of Hester's favourite foods, including a bowl of succotash, a platter of cornbread and a steaming dish of baked clams. A pot of venison stew gave off thin wisps of fragrant steam, and Ma had baked Hester's favourite cake, made with walnuts, chestnuts and honey.

Samuel reached for a crispy sliver of Jerusalem artichoke. Hester caught a flash of anger in Pa's eyes as he slapped his hand away. 'Wait for Hester to eat first,' he said.

She stared at the small feast on display. 'You cooked all of this for me?'

Martha linked her arm through Hester's and drew her towards the table. 'What is today's date, Hester?'

'The seventh day of November,' Hester replied.

'The seventh day of November,' Ma echoed. 'The anniversary of your birth.' Her expression turned solemn. 'We wanted to give thanks to God for sparing your life that day.' She bowed her head. 'May your mother's soul rest in peace.' She beckoned Hester to draw nearer. 'I know you have found it difficult since learning about the circumstances of your birth, but whatever happens from this day forward, always remember we love you and that you are as much a Trelawney as the rest of us.'

Hester nodded, wrestling with her thoughts. The anniversary of a birthday usually passed with little more than a mention, but Ma and Pa had found a reason to make her birthday a thanksgiving. Though she knew she should show gratitude, their kindness served as a reminder of all that she had lost. She wondered if in England they celebrated birthdays every year.

'I don't know how to thank you.' Hester forced a smile. 'Shall we sit and eat?'

'There's one more thing before we sit.' Pa bent to retrieve something from the floor. When he stood up, he had a large parcel in his hands. 'This arrived three weeks ago with a note instructing me to save it for today.'

Hester took the parcel from Pa and placed it on the table. 'What can it be?' She untied the string and the thick cloth binding and gasped at the gift inside.

'*The Herball, or, Generall Historie of Plantes,*' she said, reading the title on the cover. 'Written by a surgeon named John Gerarde.' Hester opened the book towards the centre and ran her fingertip over the crisp paper. Each page bore an elegant sketch and a description of a plant or flower, where to find it, its usefulness as a medicine and any additional attributes. Hester turned to the front of the book and found a folded piece of paper tucked inside. 'There's a note,' she said, opening the paper to see Giles Heale's neat script. She started reading aloud.

My dear Hester,

I asked your Pa to save this for the anniversary of your birthday. Now that you are eighteen years of age, I thought you would appreciate a manual such as this. The sketches are pleasing indeed, and the text most informative. Many of the plants will be familiar to you. Others will be of passing interest. But I hope this book brings hours of joy as a reference or source of entertainment.

Hester scanned the next paragraph, and her lips spread into a broad smile.

My contacts found your father, Hester, and I visited him myself.

'God's blood,' Pa murmured. 'Giles must have paid someone a small fortune to ensure this news arrived in time for today.'

Hester ignored Pa's interruption and continued reading aloud.

I fulfilled the promise I made to you and placed your letter in his hand. Dear girl, I hope I did right by you. Our Good Lord will determine what happens next. May He bless you and keep you.

Sincerely,

Giles Heale

Hester's mood lifted, and she grinned at the family members gathered around the table, each one watching her intently. 'This is a wonderful surprise,' she said. 'I am grateful to you all.' She folded the note and buried it deep inside the pages of the book. She wrapped the book in the cloth it had arrived in and stowed it beneath her chair. 'Let us hold hands and give thanks to the Lord for this magnificent feast.'

While Pa spoke a prayer of gratitude and asked for their food to be blessed, Hester's thoughts drifted to the future. Her father had read her letter. He knew where she lived. *Will he write back and express his joy?* she wondered. *Will he come to me on the next ship?*

CHAPTER 28

November eased into December, and Hester's mood grew dejected as no more letters arrived. One crisp afternoon, she walked along the street nearest the harbour. The youngest Mistress Eaton was heavy with child, and Hester wanted to pay her a visit to prepare her for her labour. Thick sheets of ice made the ground treacherous, and her progress was slow.

Angry voices drew her attention towards the bay where a ship lay at anchor. A small skiff was knocking against the ship, buffeted by choppy waves. A crewman was standing in the stern, grasping the rungs of a rope ladder to keep the little boat alongside. There was a gentleman leaning over the ship's gunwale and yelling at the crewman. Hester could not make out his words, but he sounded angry. A gust of wind caught his hat, and he trapped it in his hands to stop it from blowing away. Then he brandished his fist when the crewman yelled at him to climb down into the skiff. Hester smiled. What a shock the gentleman must have had seeing Plimoth for the first time! There was a small wooden pier in water too shallow for anything larger than a shallop to moor alongside and three small skiffs used as fishing boats that had been dragged to the safety of the beach. Hester wondered if the gentleman had expected a larger port such as the one in Boston. A young woman appeared at his side with a baby that looked just a few months old clasped to her chest. The gentleman took the baby and stepped aside so that his wife could descend the ladder first. The woman lost her footing as she clambered down into the skiff. Hester heard her fall with a high-pitched squeal and land in a crumpled heap. The crewman helped her to her feet, and she reached up for her baby. She made no further fuss about her fall and settled on a bench seat. Hester left them to complete the final stage of their voyage without an unwanted witness and gingerly continued on her way to visit Mistress Eaton.

When Hester left the Eaton household almost an hour later, she stepped outside onto the street to find Martha waiting for her. Martha's face was ashen, and her bottom lip quivered.

'Martha, you look chilled to the bone. How long have you been waiting?'

Martha stuffed her gloved hands into a muff and pressed the fur to her mouth and chin. 'Not long. A few minutes, perhaps. Hester, we must hurry home!'

Hester's heart skipped a beat. 'Why? Is someone hurt? Has something happened to Ma or Pa?'

Martha shook her head. 'No, nothing like that.'

'What then?' Hester started walking forward with longer strides than before. Her limp became more pronounced as the frigid temperature pierced her misshapen bones.

Martha strode beside her, her breath puffing out in clouds. 'We have visitors, Hester, and they have come all this way to see you.'

'My father?' Hester's pulse quickened as she dared to believe he had travelled so far after reading her letter.

Martha hesitated. 'Yes. I think so.'

'Well, is he, or isn't he? He must have said something to give you the idea!'

Martha's face crinkled as if she might cry. 'He introduced himself as Thomas Twisselton, but I wish it wasn't him. I can't take to him, Hester, and Lord knows what the neighbours will think when they set eyes on him.'

Of course, Martha did not want it to be him! She did not want Hester to leave for England. But Martha had grown up with her real father; it was time for Hester to enjoy time with hers.

Hester closed her eyes and thanked God for His wonderful gift. Her father must be as eager as her to reunite after so many years. He had braved a voyage across a stormy sea to find his long-lost daughter. That proved she mattered to him! Her heart swelled at the thought of seeing him, and she tried to quicken her pace.

'I am blessed, Martha,' she said. 'I will know who I am at last.'

Martha made a strange sound in her throat. 'He has brought a young woman with him, Hester. She can't be much older than you, and—.'

Hester cut her short. 'For goodness' sake, stop fretting. In a matter of moments, I will see her for myself.' *A step-*

mother close to me in age, she thought. *What great friends we shall become!*

When their home came into view, Martha slowed her steps. 'Hester, wait.' Her voice turned timid. 'Take a moment to prepare yourself. You do not know this man.'

Hester smiled at Martha. 'I do not know him *yet.*'

CHAPTER 29

HESTER THOUGHT the gentleman standing by the hearth struck an imposing figure. He was the same man she had seen on the ship, but with a calmer demeanour. She took a while to study his appearance and absorb every detail. She found him rather impressive, but also intimidating. A fashionable doublet flared at his waist, and embroidered swirls of pale grey thread seemed to dance and shimmer in the light. His sleeves were slashed many times to reveal pure white shirtsleeves beneath, and his shapeless britches were of stiff cloth and fell well below his knees. His hair was long and lustrous, the same shade of brown as hers, and a large moustache crowned his top lip, but his beard was small and pointed. *This must be the fashion in London*, Hester thought. *It will not please the Puritans here.*

'My daughter?' he said, looking Hester up and down.

Hester's breathing had quickened with excited yet nervous anticipation. 'I am Hester,' she said, eager to sit and talk.

Martha took Hester's walking stick and helped her out

of her cloak. Hester walked across the parlour, her boots tapping out her careful steps as she strained to suppress her limp. When she reached the gentleman, she lowered her head demurely and said, 'It is my pleasure to make your acquaintance.'

'I imagine it is after all this time.'

Hester heard Ma catch her breath. Ma had retreated to a corner and wore a panic-stricken expression. Pa sidled towards Ma and put his arm around her waist in a surprising public show of affection. Hester drew her gaze back to the man who had crossed a vast ocean to find her. A pleasant smell of citrus and clove emanated from him. 'Won't you make yourself comfortable at the table?' she said, gesturing towards Pa's chair. She looked over her shoulder and said to Martha, 'Our visitor needs refreshment.'

'I have already offered food and ale,' Ma said. 'Master Twisselton declined.'

Twisselton. How wonderful the name sounded as it fell from Ma's lips. 'Master Twisselton,' Hester said with a polite dip of her head. *Father!* she said in her thoughts. She glanced around the parlour seeking her father's wife. 'Mistress Twisselton,' she said, surprised to see the woman from the ship lurking in the shadow of the staircase.

Mistress Twisselton stepped forward and nodded a greeting to Hester. She still had the baby in her arms and shifted the child from one arm to the other. The baby stared at Hester with wide eyes and his lips held a little apart. Hester thought he looked a little scrawny and assumed he had not fed well during the stormy seas of his voyage.

'And who might this little person be?' Hester walked towards her stepmother and went to stroke the baby's cheek.

Mistress Twisselton stepped aside, taking the baby out of reach. 'This is Henry. I'm trying to get 'im to sleep.' Her voice sounded nervous and took on an apologetic tone. 'If you make a fuss of 'im, 'e'll not settle for the night.'

'Of course.' Hester gave Mistress Twisselton a warm smile. 'Ma's youngest, Samuel, was difficult to settle. He caused many a sleepless night.'

Mistress Twisselton did not return Hester's smile but looked furtively at her husband. Hester thought she saw a flash of fear in her eyes and wondered what might have caused it.

'Sit there,' Master Twisselton said, gesturing to Ma's fireside chair. 'The heat of the fire might send him to sleep. The rest of us have much to discuss.'

Master Twisselton approached the table and pulled out Pa's chair. After he had made himself comfortable, his gaze landed on Hester. 'Well, are you going to stand and stare at me or join me at this table?'

Hester gave a nervous laugh, then sat on the chair to his right. Ma and Pa sat opposite her on Martha's and Samuel's seats. Ma reached for Pa's hand. This was a day they had never imagined would happen. Hester knew it would be hard for them to witness the reunion.

'I have dreamed of our meeting for a long time,' Hester said, turning towards Master Twisselton. 'Since I first learned about you a full year ago.'

'I am pleased to hear it.' Master Twisselton's voice had softened. 'It was a sad day when you entered this world. Not only did I lose my beloved wife, but *she* took you away.' His narrowed eyes fixed on Ma.

'We both know that didn't happen the way you imply!' Ma held his gaze. 'Your memories of that day must be as vivid as mine.'

Hester thought she glimpsed a flush in Master Twisselton's cheeks and that his face showed a fleeting loss of composure. But he soon gathered himself together and returned his attention to Hester.

'So, tell me about yourself, Hester.'

Hester found herself lost for words. What should she tell him? Was he asking about the deformity of her foot, or her interests and ambitions? After a long pause, she said, 'Well, I have worked with Ma for many years and have become a competent midwife. I still prefer to have her reassurance with the more difficult births, but I manage alone most times.' She studied the shelf of Ma's textbooks and ledgers while she sought something else to say. Her favourite book caught her eye. 'I have an excellent knowledge of healing plants and flowers and have read John Gerarde's *Herball* from cover to cover.'

Master Twisselton raised his eyebrows. 'Midwifery is a useful skill, but I would counsel against talk of using healing herbs or you'll attract accusations of witchcraft in England.'

'But I only use my knowledge for the good of my patients. I would never wish anyone harm.' Eager to turn attention away from something that appeared to unsettle her father, Hester forced lightness into her voice. 'Please tell me about yourself. I know so very little about you.'

'It's hard to know where to begin.' Master Twisselton fiddled with the collar of his shirt. 'I was not in a good way when your mother died, Hester.' A pained expression flitted across his brow.

'Guilt will do that to a man,' Ma mumbled, just loud enough for everyone to hear.

Master Twisselton ignored her. 'I did not intend to abandon you forever, Hester. I very much wanted you in my life, and I searched for you when I was back to myself.' His mouth turned down at the corners. 'Alas! You were nowhere to be found.'

'You knew where we lived,' Ma hissed. Hester watched her knuckles whiten as she grasped the edge of the table.

Master Twisselton scowled at her. 'Not after you moved away.'

'Then you took your time to look for her. You waited over three years!'

'Desire.' Pa's voice sounded soft and calming. 'Let our guest speak with his daughter.'

The baby made a mewling sound and fussed in his mother's arms. Mistress Twisselton stood up and rocked him from side to side. She murmured words of comfort and begged him to settle.

'Please tell me more,' Hester said to Master Twisselton.

'I didn't give up on you,' he said, looking stern. 'I found the surgeon who murdered my wife—'

'He did no such thing!' Ma stood up, tipping her chair backwards and knocking it against the dresser. 'Your wife died from blood loss, as you well know. The surgeon could do nothing for her, but he saved your daughter's life.'

'Anyway,' Master Twisselton continued, ignoring Ma's interruption, 'I demanded he tell me where you had gone, and he said he did not know.'

Hester furrowed her brow. As far as she was aware, Pa and Giles Heale had exchanged regular letters for as long as she had lived in New England. What reason would Giles have had to keep that from her father?

'I scoured the length and breadth of London and then gave up all hope. And then, at a time I least expected it, I received your letter.'

Ma made a choking sound as she sat back on the chair. Hester saw that she was weeping. Pa was trying to comfort her and looked as if he might weep too.

'You will like our home,' Master Twisselton said, looking around the parlour with an expression of disdain. 'It's not as… primitive as here.'

Hester tried to see the parlour from her father's perspective. Although it was one of the largest houses in the town, it lacked fashionable charm. The table and chairs were of a simple design; the plastered walls were plain. The dresser shelves had warped with age and there were several cracks in the wood. There were glass panes in the windows, but the drapes had faded and thinned.

'Tell me about your home,' Hester said.

'I have a three-story townhouse near a street called the Strand.'

'That's not the home I recall,' Ma interjected.

Master Twisselton smiled at Hester. 'I was fortunate enough to inherit a sum of money when a childless uncle died. My luck did not run out there, for I won an inn in a wager. I wouldn't say I'm wealthy, but we live a comfortable life.' He glanced towards his wife. 'Isn't that right, my dear?'

His wife nodded at Hester. 'Yes, that's right.'

Hester tried to imagine his house standing tall and proud. There would be carriages rolling past and smart people promenading on the street he called the Strand.

'I would love to see your house,' Hester said.

'Of course you would,' Master Twisselton replied. He leaned towards her and said in a conspiratorial voice, 'And I promise you shall.'

'Over my dead body,' Ma said between sobs.

Master Twisselton fixed her with a cold, hard stare.

Hester felt a shiver pass through her. How she wished Ma would refrain from making impolite protests.

The baby started wailing. Mistress Twisselton grew distressed. 'Hush, little one. Stop now, please! There, there. Go to sleep.'

But the baby cried louder and thrashed his little fists. Master Twisselton rose from his chair and strode towards his wife. She cowered away as he loomed over her and held her baby tight. But the baby still cried and protested, filling the room with his noise.

'God's teeth, will you silence that child!'

Hester could almost taste the anger as the words fell from her father's lips. 'Perhaps his cloth needs changing,' she said, eager to restore the peace.

Mistress Twisselton lifted the baby and sniffed at his wrappings. ''T'aint that,' she said in a timid voice. 'I think 'e might be teething. Poor mite, gets in such a state.'

Master Twisselton bent forward and slapped her hard across the cheek. Hester stared with an open mouth. 'Why did you—?'

'Hush, Hester.' Pa reached across the table and rested his hand on her wrist. He gave her a gentle squeeze before letting go again.

'How often must I tell you? Make it clear to the little brat that you're the one in charge.' Master Twisselton's nostrils flared. His face turned a shade of puce. 'Must I teach the child a lesson for making such a fuss?'

Hester felt her skin go cold despite the heat of the room. Acrid bile stung the back of her throat, and she feared she might be sick. Her father was not the gentleman he tried to portray. He was a man who beat his wife and gambled with his money. He was nothing like the man she had imagined, and as she started to see him for what he really was, his clothes seemed to turn from smart to gaudy. She could not help but wonder why he had travelled so far to see her.

Master Twisselton turned to Martha. 'Would you be so kind as to show us to our chamber?'

'Your chamber?' Martha replied, looking at Ma and Pa for advice.

'You expected us to come all this way but do not offer room and board?'

'I didn't invite you,' Ma said, staring down at her hands.

'No, you didn't, did you? But my daughter did.'

Hester tried to recall the wording of her letter. She had not suggested he come to her but supposed she had implied it.

'Put them in our chamber, Martha,' Pa said, in a surprisingly calm voice. 'And put clean sheets on the bed. Ma and I will sleep downstairs for the duration of their stay.'

Martha nodded nervously. 'This way, please,' she said, inviting them to follow her up the stairs.

Hester watched them climb to the top, the baby still bawling in his mother's arms. She looked at Pa and saw sadness in his eyes as he spoke soothing words to Ma.

The bedchamber door slammed shut, and Martha descended the stairs alone. 'He said they'll change the sheets themselves,' she said, her face a mask of shock.

'What have I done?' Hester murmured, hearing her father shout at his son. The baby's wails grew louder, and Hester feared her father would strike his wife again. But then she heard her stepmother sing, and the baby's crying stopped. Hester buried her face in her hands as her own tears threatened to fall. She had brought violence into her lives. She had opened Pandora's box.

CHAPTER 30

THE NEXT MORNING, the parlour fire took a long time to draw. Smoke billowed into the room, its bitter taste catching the back of Hester's throat and sending her into a fit of coughing. She added more kindling to nurture the flames from the small pile of wood. After several minutes, the flames persisted. She threw a log onto the fire, and when it burned steadily, she returned to the kitchen to help Ma prepare the breakfast.

The family took their places at the parlour table together with their guests. Mistress Twisselton did not utter a word and kept her chin tipped towards her chest. The Twisseltons had been late to rise and blamed it on fatigue from their voyage, but Hester knew they had been awake for some time. She had heard them arguing at least an hour earlier.

The aroma of fried bacon wafted through the air and mingled with the smell of woodsmoke and freshly baked cornbread. Hester's stomach gurgled and ached for something to eat.

'Master Twisselton, may I serve you?' She extended her hand towards him.

'You may address me as Father now,' he replied, holding out his plate.

Hester's stomach roiled. Her appetite disappeared. Only the previous morning, she had longed to address him so. She loaded his plate with two rashers of bacon and a perfectly cooked egg.

'Please help yourself to the bread,' she said, passing the plate back to him.

Master Twisselton raised his eyebrows. 'This isn't enough to sustain a grown man. Give me two more slices of that delicious-smelling bacon.'

Hester had only fried enough for two slices each, so speared the rashers she would have eaten herself and dropped them onto his plate. She helped herself to a small hunk of bread and smeared it with honey, but the bread felt as dry as dust in her mouth and she found it hard to swallow. She washed the bread down with a mouthful of ale and then pushed her plate aside. Ma shuffled her chair closer to Hester's. She reached for Hester's hand and squeezed it, her action concealed by the table. Hester bit her bottom lip. Her vision blurred with tears.

'Hester, it's time you joined your proper family,' Master Twisselton said, brandishing his knife in the air. 'You've licked Trelawney plates for long enough. You're a Twisselton woman now.'

'This is Hester's home,' Pa said. His tone was polite, but his expression was not. 'She will remain with us.'

Master Twisselton raised his eyebrows. 'You have

already stolen her from me once. You will not steal her again.'

Hester stared at the table and dug her fingernail into a scratch. The wood was old and battered but it was where they played games of merels and chess, where they laughed and ate most of their meals.

Ma released Hester's other hand and reached for the pitcher of ale. She refilled Master Twisselton's cup and said, 'Why don't we ask Hester what she prefers?'

Hester threw a grateful smile at her mother. 'I would like—'

Master Twisselton cut her short. 'What the girl wants is of no consequence.' He fixed Hester with a hard, calculating stare. 'You will join our home in London. You've been absent for long enough.'

'Your lifestyle is not for Hester,' Ma said in a bitter tone.

Master Twisselton reached across the table until his pointed finger almost touched Ma's nose. 'You know nothing about me and my business matters,' he said. 'I'll thank you to not interfere.'

Pa knocked his hand down. 'I'll thank you for showing respect to my wife.'

'Respect? Your wife is a thief. She stole my beloved child and smuggled her abroad.'

Hester felt Ma stiffen. Samuel was open-mouthed. She saw Martha dig him in the ribs and tell him to close his mouth.

'Hester,' Master Twisselton said, softening his tone. 'In London, you'll never dirty your hands again from working the land.'

'I do little of that anyway,' she said, looking up to meet his gaze. 'I do a bit of weeding and tend to the herb beds, but Pa does the heavy work and Samuel helps him.'

'What we do not grow ourselves, we can purchase in the town,' Pa said. He took a swig of his ale. 'Our patients pay us in kind with food, cloth and services, or coins whenever they can.' He gave Hester a fond look. 'For a woman so young, Hester has built herself a fine reputation as a midwife and nurse. She has a promising future here and will earn a good living with her skills.'

'She will find much demand for her midwifery skills when she lives with me in London.' Master Twisselton stroked his beard between his thumb and forefinger. 'I believe we will fare very well together.'

Hester looked at Mistress Twisselton to gauge her reaction to the exchange, but Mistress Twisselton kept her eyes lowered and her head tipped down. The baby woke from his slumber and fidgeted in her arms. Hester glanced at Master Twisselton and caught a look of disgust.

'Will you excuse me for a few minutes,' Mistress Twisselton said. 'This little one needs feeding.' She lifted her head to seek her husband's approval. Hester stifled a gasp. Her left eye was bloodshot, and the surrounding skin was various shades of red, purple and blue.

Hester's eyes flitted towards Master Twisselton. He flicked his wrist to shoo his wife away to feed the restless baby and then helped himself to another hunk of bread.

'We will live well, I think, what with your midwifery earnings and the incomes from my businesses.'

'And what business income might that be?' Ma said. 'A

week's wages speculated on a bear fight or a winning wager on a cock?'

Master Twisselton ignored her and took another mouthful of cornbread.

Hester summoned the courage to speak. 'Master Twisselton…'

'Father.' Crumbs sprayed from his mouth as he spoke. Hester watched them settle on the table like large flecks of dust. 'Come on, girl, say it! After the effort you put into finding me, you must relish the reward.'

'Father.' Saying the word aloud caused Hester's chest to hurt.

'That's more like it!'

Hester traced the rim of her plate, and her fingertip found a dent. It was from Ma's best set of pewter ware but it was showing its age. It might not be perfect, but it served them well enough. 'Father, if it's all the same to you, I'd prefer to stay here.'

'And you shall!' Pa pushed his chair back from the table and rose to his feet. 'Forgive me, I must excuse myself from the table. I have patients to see.'

'A man must provide for his family by whatever means he is able, and I assure you, Trelawney, I will do the same for my daughter.' Master Twisselton took a gulp of ale. 'You've had Hester for long enough. It's my turn now. We leave for Boston the day after tomorrow and then sail onward to England.' He slapped his mug onto the table. Ale sloshed over the brim. Hester suppressed the urge to wipe it away with her napkin. 'Before we say farewell to each other, we must discuss recompense, but that can wait until later. Go! Visit your patients.'

Pa frowned. 'Recompense for what?'

Master Twisselton had a glint in his eye as he said, 'For stealing my daughter.'

Ma's face paled. 'We did no such thing!'

Master Twisselton was unperturbed. 'You took her away from England without seeking my consent. As if it wasn't already bad enough for me to have lost my wife.' He lowered his eyelids and gave a sad shake of his head. 'My poor dear Hester.'

'How dare you feign grief for a woman you disrespected!' Hester saw a nerve twitch in Ma's temple.

Master Twisselton glared at Ma. Hester thought his eyes looked a little glassy. 'She was the gentlest of women,' he said, in a voice filled with sadness. He pulled on the lapels of his jacket and took a deep breath through his nose. 'Hester has been of an age to earn money for several years now, so not only did you abscond with my daughter, but you stole an income source as well. We won't trouble ourselves with the smaller details now.' He rose from his chair and stood almost toe-to-toe with Pa. 'But we will discuss them later.'

Hester stared towards the window. Snow had fallen overnight and clung to the panes of mottled glass. *Is it snowing in London?* she wondered. *Is it warmer there than here?* The atmosphere grew oppressive, and she found it hard to breathe. Voices floated around her, but the words were indistinct.

Samuel appeared at her side and bent towards her ear. 'I don't care for your father,' he whispered. 'Don't go away to live with him. I want you to stay here.'

Hester buried her face in her hands. The truth stabbed

at her heart. She had ripped the happiness from her family home by chasing her fanciful dream. She took a few steadying breaths before raising her head. Her father was studying her, his expression full of contempt. *He does not care for me at all*, she thought, holding his gaze. *He wants me for what I might earn.* She lowered her head and closed her eyes. *May God forgive my foolishness and return him to England without me.*

CHAPTER 31

THAT NIGHT, Hester cried until her tears ran dry. She lay on her back with the darkness pressing down on her and listened to Martha breathe in and out. By dawn, Hester felt drained and light-headed, and she was dreading the day ahead. She had one last day with the parents who loved her and one more night sharing a bed with Martha. After that she would be a Twisselton on her way to England. Regret burned inside her chest. All her muscles ached. She reached across Martha to part the drapes and slide open the window shutter. Wintry daylight slipped through the glass and illuminated the bedroom. The closet doors and her travelling chest glowed with ethereal strips of silver. Hester turned her head from side to side to ease the tension building in her neck. She caught Martha looking at her; she had dark circles shadowing her eyes and her face was pale and gaunt. Martha gave Hester a quivery smile and began to weep.

'Please don't cry,' Hester said, struggling to keep her composure.

'I don't want you to go to London.'

Hester shed a few tears of her own, wringing the coverlet in her hands.

A noise from the far side of the bedchamber caused Hester to hold her breath. Someone had opened the door.

'Who's there?' Hester said in a loud whisper as the door hinges creaked. A shadowy figure stepped into the room.

'It's me.' Ma slipped into the bedchamber and pushed the door to behind her. 'I see we have all shared a restless night,' she said, perching on the edge of the bed. 'Martha, will you dress yourself and set the fires? I wish to speak with Hester in private.'

'Yes, Ma, and I'll feed the goats and chickens too.' Martha scrambled out of bed and pulled on the clothes she had worn the day before. As she tied the laces of her jacket, she said, 'Ma, please don't let Hester go.'

Ma nodded at Martha and waved her away, urging her to leave the room.

Hester pushed herself up to a sitting position and pulled the coverlet around her and Ma to shield them from the cold air. 'I'm sorry, Ma. So very sorry. My father is not the man I imagined.'

Ma put her arm around Hester and held her while she sobbed. When Hester's tears dried up again, she snuggled into Ma. She nuzzled close against Ma's neck, breathing in the smell of her skin and absorbing her selfless love. The sounds of other people rising and talking carried into the room. Muffled, terse words came from across the small landing where the Twisseltons occupied Ma and Pa's bedchamber. The slam of a chest lid silenced the feeble squeals of the baby. A volley of curses and insults caused Hester and Ma to exchange worried looks.

'Your parents had very little while they were expecting you,' Ma said. 'A small room in a run-down building, a bed, a few small pieces of furniture and a couple of pots and cauldrons. What little your father earned at work he soon frittered away. Your father is the type of man to gamble his way to wealth, but no fortune he could win would ever be enough. I fear that everything he has now will disappear again one day.'

Hester clung to Ma's arm. 'My father is the vilest of men. A gambler and a wife-beater.' She looked up at Ma's face. 'Will he beat me too?'

A tear trickled onto Ma's cheek. 'Not if I can help it.'

'You knew he was like this, didn't you?'

'I did,' Ma said under her breath.

'Why didn't you tell me?'

Ma had a faraway look in her eyes as she contemplated her answer. At last, she said, 'I knew the truth would hurt you. You deserved a better father than that poor excuse for a man. When you sent your letter to Giles, I prayed it would not reach him, but God thought it wise to bring your father to our door. I know He has his reasons, Hester, but for the life of me, I cannot determine what they are.'

How Hester wished her letter had not made it as far as London, but she knew all too well that if she had heard nothing, she would have written again. Her stubbornness was her downfall. 'Tell me what happened the day I was born, Ma. Tell me everything you recall.'

Ma released Hester from her embrace and turned sideways to face her. 'It won't be easy to hear.'

Hester swallowed. 'I know. But I want to understand why my father abandoned me, and why you did not do the same.'

'Very well.' Ma took a slow breath before speaking again. 'I have already told you how your father turned up at our house in a state of utter panic, but when I saw your mother, it was clear he had waited far too long. She had lost a lot of blood, but she wasn't ready to travail.'

'You said she had fallen, and that caused the placenta to tear.'

Ma inclined her head. 'A fall of sorts was the cause. An accident had occurred.'

'What kind of accident?' Hester asked. 'Was it caused by my father?'

'I'm afraid so.' Ma glanced towards the door. 'He had pushed her down the stairs.'

Hester gasped. 'Why?'

'Your father said he'd collected his wages that morning, then lost all his money on a cockfight, and when he told your mother, she flew into a rage. He claimed she lashed out at him and tore at his face and that he tried to defend himself by pushing her away, but she stumbled backwards and tumbled down the stairs.'

Hester saw a flicker of irritation on Ma's face. 'You didn't believe him, did you?'

'No, I did not. There wasn't a bruise or scratch on him.' Ma hesitated before continuing the story. 'Your mother was deteriorating in front of me. I knew she was going to die, and the only good that could come of that day was saving her unborn child.'

'Was that when you sent for Giles Heale?'

'It was. He wouldn't have been the nearest surgeon, but I knew he was the best. In the minutes it took for him to arrive, your mother lost more blood.'

Hester reached for Ma's hand and squeezed her fingers hard. She hoped somehow her mother had known how Ma had saved her child.

'I can stop there, Hester,' Ma said softly.

Hester tightened her grip on Ma's hand. 'I need to know the rest.'

'Very well. Your father refused to allow Giles to use his knife. By the time he consented, it was too late. We were lucky not to lose you too.' Ma drew the coverlet tighter around them. 'Your mother knew you had arrived in the world, Hester, and I believe that knowledge brought her great comfort. I held her wrist to guide her fingers to your cheek so she could feel your skin.'

Hester tried to imagine her mother's touch. 'May her spirit be with me always,' she murmured.

'I told her she had a daughter, an adorable little girl, and like I told you before, I swear your mother smiled. She passed from this world to the next knowing you would live.'

Ma fell silent as if unwilling to continue.

Hester said, 'What did my father do next?'

Ma pursed her lips and shook her head. 'Can't we end the telling there?'

'No, Ma, it's important that I know.'

Ma gave a resigned sigh. 'Your father waited outside while we attended to your mother. He grew distraught when I told him she had died. I believed his reaction was because of guilt and not because of grief. He accused me and Giles of killing his wife and said we should have let you die with her.'

'How could he say that!' Hester felt as if she had been kicked in the stomach. At first her father wished her dead, but now he wished to claim her.

'Oh, Hester, I tried to get him to look at you, but he was adamant he did not wish to. He turned and ran away from me, and that was the last I saw of him. I asked his neighbours to take you in, but each of them refused. I confess that came as a relief to me because, by then, I was eager to raise you myself.'

Hester looked at Ma through tear-filled eyes. 'I'm so pleased you did.'

'I am too. Your mother deserved her baby to have a home where her father would never beat her for a petty misbehaviour or speaking out of turn.' Ma swallowed. 'I cannot deny how much I longed for a child of my own. Your father knew where we lived, so I expected a day might dawn when he would come to claim you. Every day, my love for you grew stronger, and then I could not bear the thought of ever giving you up.'

'Is that why we came here?'

'No, but when Pa suggested we come back to Plimoth, I believed God had answered my prayers. Here, we were out of your father's reach, and I knew we could keep you.'

'Until I sent him my letter.'

Ma and Pa's bedchamber door banged. Heavy footsteps descended the stairs.

'Desire Trelawney?' Twisselton shouted. 'Where are you, woman? I need to break my fast.'

Hester trembled at the sound of his voice.

Ma gave Hester a rueful smile. 'Pa often said we should tell you what happened, but I begged him not to. I saw it as my duty to shield you from that horror. With hindsight, I was wrong. If I had told you everything, you might not have written that letter.'

Hester considered that for a moment. 'No, Ma. You did what you thought was best. I would still have believed my father could change, and I still would have wanted to meet him. But now I see him for what he really is, and I understand what you did for me.' Hester's heart raced, and she felt dizzy. 'I don't want to leave you,' she said, clinging to Ma. 'London is so far away.'

Ma drew Hester closer to her. 'Pa and I talked throughout the night. That vile man is your natural father and as such he has a legal right to claim you and take you to England, even if it's against your will. But, Hester, I promise we will do all we can to resist him.'

Thoughts tangled in Hester's mind. Her romantic dreams of a wonderful father had evaporated like steam. It was time to follow Adam's advice and acknowledge all that was good in her life. She had yearned for a perfect father, and she had one in Pa. She also had a mother who could not love her more.

'I know who I am, Ma,' Hester said. 'I'm Thomas and Hester Twisselton's child by blood, and Hester's spirit lives within me. But I'm a Trelawney in my heart and soul, and this is where I belong.'

'That's true, Hester.' Ma's eyes dimmed as she lowered her voice. 'But your father has yet to name his price. Let us pray we can reason with him.'

CHAPTER 32

THE SUN SHONE from an unencumbered sky, and the air was dry and crisp. The snow glistened as it melted, and the sea turned from grey to dark blue. Shallow waves licked the shore, whispering over the sand, and distant voices carried in the air as sailors went about their morning chores.

Hester brushed fragments of ice from the fallen tree trunk where she and Adam had sat together. She had slipped out of the house soon after breakfast, needing time to sit by herself. She perched on the tree trunk and stared at the ship that would carry her to England. Its silhouette cast a long shadow that reached across the water towards her. Hester glanced over her shoulder, looking towards the town. She tried to recall when and why she first felt she did not belong. Elizabeth Alden's wedding. Why had it upset her so that she could not dance? It had never been an issue for her before, but somehow, it had led to this – an unpleasant guest who insulted Ma and Pa and insisted that Hester live with him.

What a fool she had been! Hester had wasted so much time chasing the notion of a loving long-lost father and had disregarded everyone who showed her genuine respect and affection. She was part of a family that cherished her and who would miss her when she left. She was a respected member of the community, its youngest midwife and nurse. Hester recalled the youths who had taunted her and added to her doubts. She should have risen above their taunting instead of developing a misguided obsession that had clouded her judgement. Hester rested her gloved hand on the section of trunk where Adam had sat. She recalled the moments he had declared his love and expressed his wish to make her his wife. *Dearest Adam*. He was a man she cared about deeply, but she had denied her feelings for months.

Hester kicked the tree trunk and cried out as a searing pain shot through her lower leg. She checked the back of her boot to see if she had scuffed it and noticed the leather was dark with a fresh coating of wax. She became aware of the smell of beeswax mixed with pungent tallow. Pa must have waxed her boots the previous evening to make them waterproof and protect her feet from a soaking during her voyage to England. His kindness brought a lump to her throat. It was a typical thoughtful gesture from Pa. She wondered if Thomas Twisselton had ever done that for his wife. She doubted it very much. Her father's wife. It dawned on Hester that she did not know her stepmother's name.

'Is this seat taken?'

Adam's smooth, deep voice felt like a soothing balm to

Hester. How had she failed to realise that she loved him more deeply than as a friend?

'Good morrow, Master Phillips,' she said, feeling a bloom rise in her cheeks.

'We are friends, Hester, are we not? You must address me by my name.' Adam gave her a warm smile. They both laughed at the exchange, almost the same words they had spoken a year before.

'Please join me,' Hester said.

Adam settled beside her and fiddled with his shirt cuff. 'I heard your father has arrived in Plimoth. I assume you'll return to London with him, so I came to bid you farewell.'

'No!' Hester said, but the catch in her breath made the word sound more like a cough. She cleared her throat and thought for a moment about the words she should speak next. 'Adam, I have made the biggest mistake imaginable, and I do not know how to put it right.' She turned her head to look at him. He seemed to glow with love.

Hester fought the urge to weep but could not suppress her tears. 'My father was the reason my mother died giving birth. I didn't know, Adam. All this time, Ma kept it a secret to protect me from the truth.' She watched a man haul a cart towards a ship's tender that he had tied up securely alongside the pier. 'My father is the worst of men,' Hester said. 'My life is about to change.'

Adam shifted his position on the trunk. He reached inside his jerkin and pulled out Shadow. He lowered the squirrel to the ground and scattered a handful of walnuts. The little squirrel loped towards them. He scooped a walnut into his paws and nibbled at the nut meat. When

Adam replaced his hand on the tree trunk, his fingers brushed against Hester's glove. Heat flooded through the leather and into her hand. How she longed to embrace him! But it was too late for that. She had dismissed his declarations of love, citing a preference to leave for England.

'Is there anything I can do to help you?' Adam asked.

'I doubt it, but thank you for offering.' Hester peeled off her gloves and used one to dry her eyes. Her tears soaked into the leather, leaving a dark stain. 'My father is demanding recompense for the years I've been a Trelawney. He also expects me to work for him, serving in his inn as well as delivering babies, to earn as much money as I can.' She pressed her hand onto the tree trunk to adjust her position. The rough ridges pressed into her skin, leaving an impression. 'He hasn't said how much he wants, but staying will cost more than leaving.'

Hester's breaths grew fast and shallow as she imagined life as a Twisselton. She knew her father beat his wife. She had seen the bruises. Her father was certain to hit her like that whenever she displeased him. Her skirt started trembling as her legs shook beneath it. Bitter bile burned the back of her throat, and she found it hard to swallow. She took a few steadying breaths. The air was fresh and salty on her tongue. *London's air won't taste like this.*

'Adam,' she said, her voice thick with emotion. 'There is something you can do for me, if you are willing.'

'Hester,' he said, looking at her with a serious expression. 'I would do anything for you.'

'Even after the way I treated you, and spurned your affection?'

Adam drew his gaze away from her and looked towards the ship. 'I will not deny you hurt me with your rejections, but I knew what it meant to you to find your father.' He returned his gaze to Hester. 'I am so sorry that he's not the man you hoped he would be and that your dream has become a nightmare.'

Hester yearned for him to take her in his arms and wrap her in his affection. She loved Adam, truly loved him, with every part of her being. The thought of leaving him behind was tearing her apart.

'What I'm about to ask of you is more than I should ever ask of a person.' Hester's throat tightened. She dipped her chin towards her chest. 'But first, I need to ask if you still love me after the way I treated you.'

'I do.'

Hester raised her head. 'Do you mean it?'

'As God is my witness, I do.'

'Will you—'

'Hester—'

'You first,' Hester said.

Without hesitation, Adam said, 'Marry me!'

The very words she would have spoken herself. The churning in Hester's stomach gave way to a fluttering, and the sun seemed to shine more brightly, chasing the chill from the air. Hester interlocked her fingers with Adam's and a rush of heat passed through her. An unspoken pledge passed between them, a commitment to love one another for better or for worse.

Hester beamed at Adam. 'There is nothing I would love more than to become your Mistress Phillips and stay with you here.'

Adam raised her hand to his lips and peppered it with delicate kisses. 'So, you accept my proposal of marriage?'

Hester's eyes filled with tears of joy. 'Yes, Adam. Yes!'

CHAPTER 33

'Slow down, Hester! You'll take a tumble!' Adam chuckled as he grasped her arm.

Hester had caught her foot in a divot and tripped, tangling her skirt around her walking stick. 'I'm eager to tell Ma and Pa,' she said, beaming at Adam. 'They are both so fond of you, I know they'll welcome our news. Lord knows, they need it after all I have put them through.'

Frosty silence greeted Hester when she opened the door to her home. Grey shadows rimmed Ma's eyes as if she had been crying. Pa was pacing back and forth across the room, wringing his hands together and muttering to himself. Her father was sitting on Pa's chair at the head of the table, studying his fingernails and picking out pieces of dirt. Martha and Samuel were absent. Hester presumed Ma had sent them both on errands to spare them the discomfort of the Twisseltons' presence. The swaddled baby was fast asleep on a bundle of blankets on the wooden floor. Mistress Twisselton was sitting at the table, looking as sullen as usual. The bruise beneath her eye had darkened with an ugly slash of dark grey. Hester pitied her and her scrawny little baby. The poor little boy would never have the loving upbringing Hester had enjoyed.

'Hester, where have you been?' Ma rose from her chair by the fire and hurried across the room. She wrapped Hester in a tight embrace and kissed her on the forehead. Never had a kiss from Ma felt filled with so much love. 'We were worried about you.'

'Forgive me, Ma,' Hester said. 'I needed time to think.'

'Adam,' Ma said, ushering him back towards the door. 'You must forgive me for sending you away, but we have family matters to discuss.'

'That's why he's here,' Hester said. 'There's something he wishes to say. Tell them, Adam.'

Hester watched Adam look from Ma to Pa, willing him to speak.

Adam cleared his throat. 'Master Trelawney, I wish to declare my fondness for your daughter and ask your permission for us to wed.'

Ma crossed her hands over her chest. 'Praise the Lord,' she said.

Pa moved closer to Adam and patted his upper arm. 'That is wonderful to hear,' he said. He gave Hester a fleeting smile, but his expression turned serious again. 'Of course, you have my—'

'He will not marry my daughter,' Master Twisselton said, cutting Pa short. He fixed Adam with a mean glare and said, 'It is *my* permission you should have sought, boy, for I am the wench's father.'

Ma tightened her hold on Hester. 'Keep heart,' she whispered. 'We will try to resolve this.'

A heaviness settled in Hester's stomach. She had felt as if she were floating through the air after Adam's proposal. He was a kind, caring man who would support her work as a midwife and encourage her thirst for knowledge. He would permit her to study plants and learn more about healing herbs and flowers. Together, they would rescue squirrels and birds and offer a home to unwanted children. A future with Adam was far removed from a future as Master Twisselton's daughter. Hester had to do everything possible to avoid going to England.

'Father?' She limped towards Master Twisselton while considering the words she should use. Forcing courage into her voice, she said, 'Yesterday, you implied you would accept money, a compensatory payment for not taking me with you.'

'Twisselton has already named his price,' Pa said, sounding wretched. 'It's a sum we cannot raise.'

Hester felt as if the floor was swaying. She grasped the back of a chair. 'May I ask how much?'

Pa's face creased into a scowl. He pointed at Master Twisselton. 'That man would have worked you from five years old, clearing tables and washing dishes.'

Hester did a quick calculation in her head. As a small child doing menial tasks, she would not have brought much value, but from her teenage years her father would have worked her harder to save paying wages to other people. She estimated a sum of ten pounds per year from age five years to eighteen. 'One hundred and thirty pounds,' she muttered. An eye-watering total.

'That would be no recompense for the pain of losing my daughter.' Master Twisselton glowered at Hester. 'Nor the money you would have earned while living with me in London. It will take many years to recover what the Trelawneys took from me. I've been without you for eighteen years, and my dear wife too.' He looked at Mistress Twisselton. His eyes were cold and hard. 'No one could ever replace my dear, sweet Hester.'

Hester watched Mistress Twisselton for her reaction. Her father's comment must have hurt. Mistress Twisselton shared a meaningful glance with Ma but maintained her silence.

Master Twisselton moved to Hester's side and grasped her shoulders, turning her to face him. 'There are so many years to make up for, I might never give permission for you to marry.' He released her and looked down his nose towards her boots. His lips widened into an ugly smile. 'No man in his right mind would want you, anyway.'

'I do.' Adam's voice was clear and confident as he strode towards Hester's father. 'Is there anything we can do to persuade you to let her stay?'

Master Twisselton's eyes glinted with mirth. 'Goodness me, you are a cocksure young man, but it's clear you were not listening. Either I take the girl home with me,' he jerked his head towards Ma and Pa, 'or they agree to my price.' He took a step towards Hester. She took a step back. He carried the smell of stale tobacco, and it made her stomach churn. 'My daughter is precious to me,' he said in a syrupy tone. 'But if you wish to keep her, I'll accept three hundred pounds.'

A chill settled over Hester as the reason for her father's visit became clearer than before. He considered her only as a financial transaction and not a beloved child of his blood.

'We don't have that kind of money,' Ma said. 'At least not in the house.' Her voice turned brittle. 'And it's more than our home is worth.'

'Pa? Is there nothing you can do?'

Pa looked wretched as he shook his head. 'I'm sorry, Hester. Coins are scarce in a colony such as this. I could borrow from our dearest friends, but their situation is much the same as ours, and your father has already made it clear he will refuse wampum and pieces of eight.'

Master Twisselton drummed his fingers on the table. 'Indian beads and Spanish coins hold no appeal for me. I'll take the longer-term investment of Hester earning instead.'

Hester felt her legs buckle. She sat on a chair and buried her face in her hands, wishing she could disappear. It was bad enough confronting the reality of the beast that was her father, but to see the distress she had wrought on Ma and Pa was more than she could bear. She had no money of her own – she had given it all to a sailor. Not that the meagre handful of coins would have altered her imminent future. Ma and Pa rarely had coins in the house, and even if they agreed to sell their home, it would be hard to find a buyer. And where would they live? Hester had set her future in stone when she asked Giles to find her father. She had no choice but to resign herself to a life of drudgery and cruelty.

Master Twisselton clapped his hands. 'Enough pathetic maudlin, daughter! Pack your clothes and trinkets. We leave on the morrow.'

Hester dragged herself up from the chair, struggling to find her balance. Her lungs burned; her heart ached. Her vision blurred with tears. She turned to look for Adam, eager for one last glimpse of his face. But all she saw was a flash of his cloak as he slipped out into the street. The latch made a loud click as he closed the door behind him.

Hester grasped the handrail and made her way upstairs, facing a life of punishment for her selfish choices. She packed her travelling chest with shifts and kirtles, and the mirror that had been Ma's. Then she fell to her knees and prayed, begging God to look after her loved ones when she left New England's shore.

CHAPTER 34

MELANCHOLY WEIGHED down on Hester as she tried to keep up with the pace. Her legs grew heavy and her foot burned as she negotiated drifts of fresh snow and thick patches of ice. Master Twisselton took long strides beside the horse and cart that carried their belongings. His wife carried the baby, holding him close to her chest. Pa, Ma, Martha and Samuel followed along behind. Hester could hear Martha and Samuel murmuring words of comfort to each other, but Ma and Pa said nothing and stared resolutely ahead. Hester assumed they had come to terms with her imminent departure – perhaps they had expected it since learning Giles had found her father.

When they reached the harbour, Master Twisselton paid the horse's owner. Two sailors came forward to take the chests and trunks and carried them towards a shallop tied up alongside the pier.

Hester squinted to read the name of the ship that would carry her to England. *Unity*, she read to herself. *If only*. She turned around to face the town of Plimoth where it clung to the hillside. People were emerging from their houses and gardens and thronging the streets. She had hoped to see Adam rushing towards her to say a last farewell, but her spirits sank even further when he was nowhere to be seen. Pa joined Hester on one side, Ma on the other. Hester felt a rush of love for them both, and then she started weeping.

'I'm sorry, Hester,' Pa said, his eyes brimming with tears. 'We did everything we could think of to try and keep you here.'

Hester was too distraught to speak.

A member of the ship's crew called out in a booming voice for all passengers sailing to Boston and London to make their way to the shallop.

'No!' Martha cried out. 'Please, not yet!'

Samuel pulled a sad face. 'I'll miss you, Hester,' he said.

Hester grasped Ma's arm. 'Please, Ma, do something! I don't want to go!'

'Be brave, my love.' Ma pointed towards the town. 'Look over there.'

Hester's spirits lightened. Adam was sprinting towards her. When Adam reached the wooden pier, Hester threw her stick to the ground. She wrapped her arms around him and pressed her cheek against his neck, relishing the feel of her skin against his and his leathery, masculine scent.

'I knew you would come,' she said. 'But my heart will break when we say our farewells.'

'You will not leave Plimoth today,' Adam said, breathless from his exertion.

Hester released him, not daring to believe him. 'Adam, do not taunt me with those words.' She looked for Pa and saw him talking to Master Twisselton with a downcast expression. When Pa shook his head, Hester said, 'Oh, Adam, my fate is settled. We cannot pay my father's demands.'

'Calm yourself, sweeting. There must be something we can do.'

Hester felt a rush of heat spread from her head to her feet. It was the first time Adam had used an endearment. She did not want it to be the last.

Adam retrieved her walking stick and nodded towards the beach. 'Look over there, Hester, and see who has turned out for you.'

A crowd had gathered on the shoreline – Hester's friends and neighbours. Some raised their hands to acknowledge her while others dabbed their eyes. Hester's heart fluttered. So many people were there to wish her well.

'Hester! Come here!' Master Twisselton's voice echoed around the harbour. A herring gull swooped down from the sky and landed by his shoe. It lurched forward with its beak open as if intending to peck his calf, but her father went to kick the bird and it flew to freedom instead.

Hester's supporters drew closer like a moving defensive wall. She could see that their expressions were full of concern for her. A new thought took root in her mind. Perhaps she could use their presence to alter the course of her fate. Her own little army ready to fight for her cause. Her legs quaked beneath her skirts, knocking her knees together. She needed to act fast. She took a few steadying breaths and then addressed the crowd.

'Friends!' Hester shouted above a cacophony of voices. 'Friends!' she shouted again, but louder this time. The noise began to subside. 'I thank you heartily for coming here to bid me farewell, but I want to make it known to you that I do not wish to leave this town.' She pointed at her father. 'He insists on taking me, though it be against my will.' The men, women and children on the beach all seemed to hold their breath. Hester took it as a sign of their goodwill. 'He is my natural father, but he's never been a father to me. He abandoned me after I was born but now wants me for a slave.' Mutterings passed through the crowd. A few mouths fell open. 'He is the cruellest of men,' Hester added. 'He even beats his wife.'

Master Twisselton clapped his hands. His lips twisted with disdain. 'My daughter's speech is over now. It's time you returned to your homes. Come, Hester, we must board the ship.'

Hester's hands turned clammy. Her breath came fast and shallow. She could see her friends and neighbours exchanging frantic words, but none of them stepped forward. Hester turned back towards her family. 'Pa, what shall I do?'

'Board the ship with me,' Master Twisselton said, grasping her by the arm.

'Don't touch her!' Adam knocked Master Twisselton's arms away. Master Twisselton clenched his fists. Adam raised his eyebrows. 'A man who lifts nothing heavier than dice should not choose a blacksmith for a fight.'

Master Twisselton's mouth twitched as if he would

make a retort, but Hester saw him look Adam up and down and decide his own scrawny frame was no match. His failure to incite a fight stimulated the crowd.

'Hester's right, that man is cruel,' yelled Mercy Bradford, stepping forward. 'We can all see the bruise on his poor wife's face. Hester deserves better than him. She should stay here with us!'

'Mercy, is your father here?' Hope surged through Hester's veins. Mercy's father knew the law and might be able to help.

'Aye, I'm here,' the governor said, striding onto the pier.

Master Twisselton looked him up and down. 'And who the hell are you?'

'My name is William Bradford. I'm the governor of this town.'

'I have no business with the town's governor. Come on, Hester. Let us put an end to this ridiculous scene and make our way to the ship. You too, wife.'

Mistress Twisselton did not move. She stood next to Pa, her posture stiff and her eyes flitting between her husband and Governor Bradford. Her gaze drifted towards Hester. Hester mouthed 'Keep heart.'

Hester cleared her throat. 'Governor Bradford, please clarify for me, is there anything written in law that says that I must board that ship?'

'Of course there is!' Her father spoke through gritted teeth. She saw his fingers curl. 'You're a Twisselton not a Trelawney,' he said. 'You're bound by the laws of England to do as your father says.'

Hester looked at the governor. 'But we are not in England. Does he hold the same rights here?'

The governor shook his head. 'Absolutely not. If you do not wish to board that ship, he cannot force you against your will.'

Master Twisselton was apoplectic. 'My lawyer would disagree.'

'Is your lawyer here with you?' asked the governor, squinting towards the ship. 'No? I thought as much. And anyway, a London lawyer has no jurisdiction in this colony. It is I and my council who handle matters of the law. As Hester's legal counsel, I confirm her home is here.'

Hester's heart was beating so hard she feared it might burst.

'I hope you don't mind,' Adam whispered, his breath warm against her cheek, 'but last night I went to his house and told him everything I know.'

Hester reached for his hand and squeezed it hard. 'I'm glad you did.'

It was Pa who spoke next. 'Thomas Twisselton, I held my tongue while you were a guest in my home, but now I wish to make it clear – your visit was unwelcome, and you will not cross our threshold again. Hester is more my daughter than she will ever be yours.' He stepped towards Master Twisselton and prodded him in the chest. 'Remind me how much money you lost the day that Hester was born. A full week's wages, was it not? And because your wife disapproved, you pushed her down the stairs.'

'I did not!'

'Yes, you did,' Ma spoke with a cool edge to her voice.

'You confessed as much when I asked what had caused your wife so much pain.' She lowered her voice and added, 'The poor love was in agony and as good as bled to death.'

'You had three years to find Hester before we boarded a ship for here.' Pa drew himself to full height and towered over Hester's father. 'Three years to claim her and raise her yourself.'

Hester released Adam's hand. 'He could have found me after that, Pa. He knew where the surgeon lived and could have asked for our address.'

'I wasn't ready,' her father blurted out.

Hester recalled her father saying he had approached the surgeon to ask where she lived. She could not help but notice that he did not make the same claim again.

'Master Twisselton!' One of the ship's officers gesticulated wildly. 'You must board now!'

'Go!' said Governor Bradford. 'You don't belong here.'

'I deserve compensation for their absconding with my daughter.' Master Twisselton seemed lost and vulnerable. An hour before, Hester would have feared he would strike Pa or the governor, but now he looked diminished to a weasel of a man.

Governor Bradford moved towards Master Twisselton until the tips of their shoes were almost touching. 'I have considered the events that have occurred, and it is my opinion that when you received Hester's letter, you tried to turn her curiosity to your advantage and took the biggest gamble of your life. But I'm pleased to say your journey to Plimoth was a complete waste of time and money. Hester has seen you for the man you are and has declared her wish to stay here.' In a stern voice, he added, 'You, however, must be on your way. Your ship is ready to sail.'

Master Twisselton scowled. 'I won't be sorry to leave this Godforsaken place. Come, wife, let us join the ship and settle into our cabin.'

'She's staying here too,' Hester said. 'Her and her little boy. That's right, isn't it, Pa?'

Pa smiled at Hester. 'If that's what she would like.'

Mistress Twisselton showed a flicker of defiance. 'It is,' she said in a soft but determined voice.

Ma sidled up to Mistress Twisselton. 'You and your son are welcome to make your home with us.'

Master Twisselton's face turned puce. 'She's not staying with you!'

But Mistress Twisselton stood her ground, much to Hester's delight. Bravado burned in her eyes as she spoke louder than before. 'I am not your wife, Thomas, and our son was not born of love.' She turned towards Ma. 'Mistress Trelawney, I'll work 'ard to pay our way. I'll do anything you ask.'

The baby turned his head towards Hester and gave her a gummy smile. *That little boy is my half-brother*, she thought. *We share the same blood*.

'You can keep my daughter, but you're not having my son.' Master Twisselton reached out to snatch the baby from Mistress Twisselton's arms, but Hester stepped between them. He tried to shove her out of the way, but she jabbed his shin with her stick.

'If you take my brother with you, he'll suffer at your

hands.' She looked towards Governor Bradford. 'Please say he can stay here too.'

The governor nodded and cleared his throat before addressing Master Twisselton again. 'You have struck a young woman's face while on colony land. We do not tolerate such violence here and would prosecute such an offence.' The governor's woollen cloak blew open with a bitter gust of wind. He pulled it tighter around himself and then continued to speak. 'The woman and child you brought with you are free to remain in this town. You, sir, have a choice. You may face a trial before me and my councillors for violence and extortion, or you may board that ship today and never visit this colony again.'

The ship's master was striding towards them, yelling Twisselton's name.

Governor Bradford gave a nonchalant shrug. 'It seems you have mere moments to make your choice.'

With an angry glare at Hester and a sneer for the woman he had called his wife, Master Twisselton turned his back and scurried along the pier. Noisy conversations broke out along the beach, and the atmosphere turned jubilant as they watched Twisselton board the shallop and head out towards the ship.

Adam drew Hester to him, and she sank into his embrace. Never had she felt so loved by him, her family and her community. When she pulled away from Adam, she saw Pa with Henry in his arms. He was pulling funny faces and making the little boy laugh. He hugged the child to him and pressed his cheek to the little boy's head. Hester imagined that was how he had held her when she was a tiny girl.

The governor was beaming at the Trelawney family group, now swelled in number by an extra woman and child. 'Seeing as you weren't married to that vile man, your name is not Twisselton,' he said. 'For the sake of the town records, how do you wish to be known?'

The young woman blushed at the governor's question. 'I was married for a little under a year to a man who worked for 'im,' she said. 'Caught a fever and died, 'e did, so Twisselton took me in. Said 'e would take care of me, but 'e did no such thing.'

'Your husband's name?' the governor persisted.

'Newnham,' she replied. 'My name is Sarah Newnham.'

'Welcome to Plimoth, Mistress Newnham.' Governor Bradford donned his hat and strode towards the town.

Hester looked at the people nearest her, the family known as Trelawney. 'This is unity,' she murmured. 'It's more than a name on a ship.' She watched the shallop float away from the pier. 'Pa!' she cried. 'Our trunks!'

'Let them go,' Ma said. 'Their contents can be replaced in time, but you, Hester, cannot.'

'Ma's right,' Pa said, smiling at Hester. Addressing the rest of his family, he said, 'It's time we all went home.'

Adam and Hester lingered at the rear of the group and walked hand-in-hand.

'Is it true what the governor said?' Hester asked, reflecting on Governor Bradford's words. 'London lawyers have no jurisdiction here? Could my father really have faced a trial?'

Adam grinned at her. 'I don't know. I'm not sure the governor knew for certain, but it doesn't matter now. The important thing is that your father will trouble you no more.'

Hester drew them to a halt and turned to look towards the bay. The ship was already under sail, gliding towards a shimmering horizon. Hester felt a lightness inside, and a rising bubble of joy. For the first time in a very long while, she knew where she belonged. And she felt complete.

CHAPTER 35

HESTER TIGHTENED her grip on her walking stick as they approached a shaded section of road. The sun had partially melted the ice, but it had refrozen into a wide, slick sheet. Adam squeezed her arm against his. The simple gesture of reassurance made Hester's heart swell with love. The family home came into view, and Hester's legs grew weak. All her muscles trembled, and a thickness filled her throat. When Hester and Adam stepped inside, Ma, Pa, Martha and Samuel all whooped with joy. They each took turns embracing her and joyfully declared their relief that she would stay in Plimoth.

Sarah gave her a warm smile. 'Welcome 'ome. Praise the Lord, neither of us is on that ship with Thomas.'

Hester returned her smile. 'Welcome home to you too, sister. May you find peace and happiness here.'

Hester looked around the parlour, a room she had thought she would never see again. The familiarity engulfed her like a comforting cocoon. The wooden table and chairs glowed in the wintry sunlight. Books and journals lined the shelves, ordered according to their use. There was a shelf for household ledgers, another for medical journals and texts, and Hester saw her own ledger stowed next to Ma's. *How fortunate I am*, she thought, *to have a mother like Ma. She has nurtured and taught me and made me who I am. May my dear mother rest in peace knowing that I am loved.* Hester reached out to lift her ledger down from the shelf. She had forgotten to put it in her travelling chest along with her trinkets and clothes. She opened the cover and turned to the most recent entry – details of a pregnant woman who was young and afraid. Hester had promised to revisit her soon to check on her and the unborn babe. Now, Hester understood true fear and felt qualified to give the young woman all the support she would need. Hester closed the journal and returned it to the shelf. 'It must have known that I'd come home,' she said, stroking the journal's spine.

'I'm starving,' Samuel declared, marching into the parlour carrying a platter of fragrant roasted duck, nuts and chunks of crumbly cheese. 'Ma wouldn't let me break my fast earlier. She said I had to wait until after you left.' He gave Hester a gap-toothed smile. 'I'm heartily glad you're still here.'

'As am I,' Hester replied. She plucked a morsel of cheese from the platter and popped it into her mouth. The cheese was salty on her tongue and made her mouth water. Realising she had eaten nothing since early the previous day, Hester scooped up a handful of nuts and another lump of cheese. Everyone took their places at the table. Pa poured cups of small beer. Ma led a prayer to thank God for returning Hester to her family. Hester said a loud 'Amen'. Next, Ma asked God to bless their new sister, Sarah, and her little boy, known as Henry Newnham.

Samuel was quick to respond with 'Welcome, new baby brother!'

Hester felt a rush of pride at her brother's ability to open his arms so easily to new family members. Ma and Pa had taught him well, just as they had taught her and Martha. Hester vowed to stop defining herself by her blood, appearance and limitations. She sneaked a sly peek in Adam's direction. His eyes were closed, his hands were raised and he was murmuring his thanks to God for saving Hester from going to England.

Pa's stomach gurgled. Laughter rippled around the table.

'Time for this family to eat,' Hester said. 'Let us celebrate our good fortune.'

As everyone feasted on meat, cheese, nuts and cornbread, Hester looked from one family member to the other, drinking in the features that made each of them unique. Of course, Ma and Pa's love for her was not the same as the love they had for her siblings. They did not love her more or less, but they loved her as their daughter. *This is where I belong,* she thought, *until I have my own home with Adam.*

Ma let out a horrified squeal. 'Dear God, there's a squirrel on the table!' She grabbed a serving trencher, spilling food as she raised it ready to swat the unfortunate little creature.

Hester scooped Shadow out of harm's way before the

trencher crashed down onto the table. 'Please don't be mad, Ma. This is Shadow. He's one of Adam's rescues.'

Ma had broken into a sweat and was fanning herself with her hand. 'Remove that animal at once, Adam. We've dealt with enough vermin for one day!'

'Forgive me, Mistress Trelawney,' Adam replied, smiling. 'Shadow forgot his manners.'

'He won't cause any harm, Ma.' Hester passed Shadow to Adam. 'He's like an animal version of me. The poor thing cannot fend for itself.'

'At least keep it out of my sight.' Ma pulled a horrified face as Adam stroked the squirrel's tail. She kept her gaze fixed on Shadow until Adam concealed him beneath his jerkin. 'You are more than capable of fending for yourself, Hester,' Ma said. 'Never let me hear you compare yourself to that creature again!'

Henry stirred in a corner of the room, where he had been sleeping in the old Trelawney cradle. Sarah went to rise from her chair, apologising for his disturbance.

'No need to fret, Sarah,' Ma said. 'I'll see to the little one.'

'Thank you, Mistress Trelawney. I don't think 'e needs feeding yet. Maybe 'e wants attention.' Sarah lifted her cup to her lips. Hester noticed her hand was trembling.

'Sarah, it has been quite a morning for you too,' Hester said. 'But you can put it behind you now.'

Sarah looked towards Ma. 'I lost my ma when I was a little girl. Can't remember 'er now. Not 'ow she looked or the sound of 'er voice. I sorely wish I could. My aunt took me in and raised me, but she was mean and spiteful. She made it clear she didn't want me but saw it as 'er Christian duty. I'm so grateful to you all for taking me into your 'ome, and my little boy too.' She caught her breath before adding, 'I never 'ad a brother or sister, Hester, so to hear you call me sister earlier… 'tis the kindest thing you could have done.'

Ma returned to her seat at the table, rocking Henry back to sleep. 'I believe you'll soon settle here, Sarah, and it will feel as much your home as it is all of ours.'

That's love, Hester thought. *It's opening your heart to someone else, connected by blood or not.* 'I'm proud to be a Trelawney,' she said.

Pa reached across the table and squeezed her fingers. 'I'm proud to have you as my daughter.' He smiled at each of his children. 'The way you all care for each other is a special kind of love. Always treasure that.'

'You won't be a Trelawney for much longer, Hester.' Ma passed Henry to her.

The baby opened his eyes wide, and Hester thought he might grizzle. But he grasped her finger in his little hand and closed his eyes again.

'You'll make a wonderful mother one day,' Sarah said to Hester.

Hester rocked Henry back and forth. 'God willing,' she replied.

'Sarah, it's time to make yourself useful,' Ma said, rising from the table. 'Help me clear the dishes away and then we will all plan a wedding.'

CHAPTER 36

'Hester!' Pa's urgent voice carried upstairs to the bedchamber.

Hester hurried towards the door, her left foot throbbing every time her boot struck the floorboards.

'Yes, Pa?'

'I need you to come with me to attend to a woman in labour.'

She could tell from the tone of his voice that there was no time for questions. When she reached the bottom of the stairs, she grasped her delivery bag. Pa handed Hester her walking stick and draped her heavy woollen cloak around her shoulders.

Outside, the sky was grey. The sun was low in the sky.

'We have a long walk ahead of us, Hester, but we must make haste. A girl on one of the farmsteads has been labouring since yesterday.' Pa took the delivery bag from her and set off through the town. His route took them up the hill and through one of the old palisade gates.

While Hester hobbled as fast as she could to keep pace

with Pa, different scenarios swirled through her mind. Was the baby a breech presentation? Had a leg or an arm entered the birth canal first? Might the mother have lost too much blood? Did she lack the energy to push?

When they reached the top of another hill, Pa stopped to allow Hester to catch her breath. 'You're doing very well,' he said. 'Are you in a lot of pain?'

Hester shook her head. Concern for the labouring mother pushed her own discomfort to the back of her mind.

Pa pointed to a farmstead in the distance. 'That's where we are going.'

The main house appeared small because of the distance from where they were standing. There were three barns behind the house, and neat fields of crops spread out before it. Men and women moved in rows, working in silence. Hester assumed they were planting. But the observation that struck her as odd was that no smoke rose from the chimney.

'I'm ready to continue, Pa,' Hester said, no longer gasping for air.

When they reached the farmhouse, there was no one to greet them at the door. Hester took a deep breath and caught the stench of rotten fish guts wafting from the fields. Pa knocked three times before the door creaked open.

'You here for the girl?' A mean-looking woman gave Hester a critical stare. Her pinched face and narrowed eyes looked as cold as her house. 'Is this your wife?'

'My daughter,' Pa replied. 'She is more than capable of handling any situation.'

The woman sniffed. 'I doubt that.'

'The mother-to-be?' Hester asked. 'Where might I find her?' She started untying the lace of her cloak when the woman raised her hand to stop her.

'You'll want to keep that on.' The woman barged past Hester, knocking against her on purpose. 'Whores do not cross my threshold.'

'I'm not a whore!' Hester was indignant.

'She doesn't mean you,' Pa said coolly.

'This way.' The woman took them back outside and across the yard to the smallest barn.

When Hester stepped inside, she was unprepared for the sight that greeted her. The interior of the barn was dingy, with only two tallow candles lighting a narrow animal pen. The smell of rotten hay was strong, and Hester tasted thick dust in the air. A young indigenous woman lay on her back on a thin layer of straw. A ragged blanket covered her legs and large distended belly. Her blood-soaked skirt had already been removed and lay in a heap in a corner of the stall. Her ripped shirt displayed bruised arms and a festering sore on her wrist.

'What's her name?' Hester asked, easing herself down onto the earthen floor.

'How should I know?' the woman replied. 'My husband manages the workers. All I do is cook their food.'

Hester tapped the pregnant mother's cheek. It was cold and slick with sweat. 'Can you open your eyes for me?' she said. She tapped her cheek a second time, harder than before. Still, no response. Hester grasped the young mother's wrist, willing herself to locate a pulse. She moved her fingers to the young woman's neck and pressed deep into her skin. The pulse was difficult to detect, but Hester felt it fast and weak beneath her finger-tips. 'Bring me hot water and linens,' she barked at the woman who owned the farm. 'And please be quick about it.'

'It won't be quick,' the woman replied. 'I'll have to get the fire burning first.' She jerked her head towards the woman lying unmoving on the straw. 'This laggard let it go out.'

When Hester and Pa were alone in the barn, Hester peered under the blanket.

'She's lost a lot of blood, Pa. I fear we are too late.'

Hester uncovered the mother's abdomen and felt for the contours of the baby. As she traced the outline of its back, an elbow pressed towards her, stretching the already taut skin. 'The baby's still alive,' she said. She sat back on her haunches, wondering how to proceed. 'The child is lying across her belly, so she won't go into proper labour.' Hester gave a sad shake of her head. 'I wish Ma were here with us. She'd know what to do.'

Pa knelt beside Hester. 'You know what to do. Take a moment to consider the situation. What do you think should happen next?'

Hester pinched her lips together, reflecting on the texts she had read and all of Ma's old notes. 'It's too late to turn the child,' she said. 'The baby won't come out.'

Pa's expression turned grim. He pressed his fingertips to the young woman's neck. 'Her heartbeat is fading.'

Hester held the back of her hand over the young woman's mouth. 'Her breaths are so shallow, Pa, it's hard to feel them at all.' A heaviness pressed against Hester's temples. 'They waited too long to send for us. Is there any hope of saving the mother?'

'I'm afraid not.' Pa pressed into the woman's neck again, rechecking her pulse. 'If we are to do anything, we need to act fast.'

Hester's stomach twisted, and her mind went blank. 'Pa, I don't know what to do!'

Pa squeezed her shoulder. 'You do, Hester. You do.'

At that moment, Hester realised these were similar circumstances to her own birth. Something violent had taken place and started the mother's labour before its natural time. She reached into her delivery bag and pulled out a knife. The candlelight caught the blade and sent a flash of golden light towards Hester's eyes.

'Will you cut her open, Pa? I'll see to the babe.'

Pa nodded his assent and swapped positions with Hester.

'Where's the hot water? And I need a large cloth to wrap the child.' Hester fumed as she glanced towards the door of the barn.

'There's no time to wait,' Pa said. He slipped off his black physician's cloak. 'Use this instead.'

Hester had to look away when Pa pressed the knife into the mother's taught belly. She clasped the young woman's cool, clammy hand, murmuring words of reassurance even though she knew full well the woman could not hear her. The unfortunate mother's fingers did not even twitch as the blade sliced through her skin. Time seemed to slow down as Hester processed what was going on around her. A young woman, unconscious, having her child ripped out of her belly. She prayed to God to save the child, and to allow the young woman to pass peace-fully and unaware of pain.

'It's up to you now, Hester.'

Hester fought a wave of nausea as she stared through the large wound and saw the baby's back. She had been right about its position. 'Lord, please help me,' she murmured as she eased her fingers through the gaping hole and into the woman's womb.

Hester fought to clear her thoughts of the horror of the situation and focused her attention on easing the baby from its tight confinement. As soon as the baby was free, she laid it on Pa's cloak. Pa quickly tied the cord with two threads and cut between them with Hester's knife. The child was limp and lifeless, so Hester blew across its face and rubbed its body with her palms. The tiny baby drew a shallow breath and made a little sound. Hester massaged the baby's chest and blew on its face again. The baby took a gasp of air, then gave a feeble cry.

Hester and Pa exchanged relieved smiles, as Hester wrapped the child. Her smile soon faded. 'The mother?' she asked.

Pa's expression turned solemn, and he shook his head. Hester said a prayer for her soul and recalled something Ma had once said. She took the mother's limp hand in hers and swept the fingertips over the baby's brow.

'You have a beautiful baby,' Hester said.

'Boy or girl?' Pa asked, covering the woman's body with the tatty old blanket.

'A little girl,' Hester replied, pitying the scrawny child.

'I brought your water and linens,' the farmer's wife said, lowering a pail and slopping water onto Hester's skirt. She looked at the deceased young mother. 'Looks like I'm too late. I asked the other girls her name. They all said they didn't know. Said this one never uttered a word after my husband brought her here to work.'

'This is her daughter.' Hester held the bundle towards the old woman.

The woman raised her palms to Hester. 'A babe's no good to me. We have enough mouths to feed.' Her lips twisted, and she wrinkled her nose at the deceased mother. 'You should have let them die together.'

'Might one of the other women raise her?'

'You think someone else would take that brat as their own?' The woman rolled her eyes. 'Do what you want with the child,' she said. 'But let me know when you've finished with the woman. We'll sort her out.'

The baby gave another mewling cry. 'What do I do with her?'

'Not my problem,' the woman said. She turned and marched out of the barn.

Hester tightened her grip on the bundle. *Was this how it was for me? An absent father, a dead mother and other women refusing to help me simply because I was different.* She felt a surge of emotion for the tiny little girl. *Is this how Ma felt when she delivered me?*

'What will you do with this little girl, Hester?' Pa asked, stroking the baby's cheek

The dim light of the barn seemed to grow brighter. Hester's thoughts cleared. 'The child deserves to live, Pa, and she needs a loving home.' She kissed the baby's forehead. 'We will call you Hope, sweeting, and you shall be my "Chosen One". When Adam and I marry, you will share our home.'

'Of course she will,' Pa murmured.

'Adam and I will raise her, Pa, like you and Ma raised me.'

Pa smiled. 'What do you think Adam will say? Do you think he will approve?'

The baby was delicate and vulnerable, and not much larger than Shadow. Hester met Pa's tender gaze. 'Adam will love her and care for her in the same way you have always loved me.'

CHAPTER 37

MA DABBED her rose perfume on Hester's throat and neck. She stepped back to look at her. 'You are beautiful,' she said.

Hester felt her cheeks glow. She smoothed her new blue skirt with her palms. The lightweight wool was cool against her skin despite the warmth of the summer day.

Ma lifted a package from Hester's bed and opened the linen wrapping. 'My old lace collar would not do for today, even if you had permission to wear it, but I hope you will find this one just as pleasing.'

Hester lifted out the collar and angled it towards the light streaming through the window. Ma had stitched a neat ruffle to the edge, each fold perfectly straight and as narrow as Hester's little finger. The white linen was of good quality and starched to keep its shape. A lump rose in Hester's throat. Ma was always so busy, yet she had found time to stitch the collar while keeping it a secret. 'I love it, Ma. Thank you.'

Ma draped the collar around Hester's shoulders and

pinned it to her bodice. 'There,' she said, taking a step back. 'Your wedding outfit is complete.'

Hester raised her mirror and held it at arm's length. She stroked the ruffle edge of the collar, feeling each fold flick against her fingertip. 'I shall treasure this forever,' she said.

Ma stood behind her and rested her chin on Hester's shoulder. Hester tilted the mirror until the filigree edging framed their faces. They both smiled.

'We might not be of the same blood, Hester, but you are, and always have been, my beloved daughter.'

'I know, Ma.' Hester swallowed. 'Can you forgive me for causing so much distress?'

'My dear, there is nothing to forgive.' Ma swept a tear from Hester's cheek with a delicate sweep of her fingertip. 'There was so much we did not tell you, and it was your right to learn the truth, but let us put all that behind us now and concentrate on what lies ahead.'

Hester pointed to their reflection. 'Look, Ma, do you see it? There's a likeness we share. We both have the same glint in our eyes of joy, compassion and love.'

'I see it.' Ma pressed her cheek to Hester's. 'Remember this image, Hester. A mother and daughter sharing a precious moment. Every time you look in the glass, remember how much I love you.'

Voices drifted up the stairs and into the bedchamber. The words were too muffled to hear, but their excitement was clear.

'It sounds like the magistrate has arrived with your betrothed.' Ma took the mirror from Hester. 'We should join them.'

The voices fell silent as Hester descended the stairs. Adam was waiting for her at the bottom and reached up to take her hand. They exchanged a fond look as guests shuffled out of their way, parting like the sea for Moses to let them walk across the room. As they stood before the magistrate, Hester surveyed all their guests – the family members, friends and neighbours who had gathered to watch them wed. Adam's mother stood with his brothers and Lydia, holding her sleeping grandson. Adam's sister and her husband stood behind them, their baby daughter's coppery hair glowing like the setting sun. Ma and Pa's dearest friends, Priscilla and John Alden, stood beside Adam's family, and John Alden held a baby of their own. Martha and Samuel were with them, both dressed in their Sunday best. Martha had Hope in her left arm and pressed her right palm to her chest. Hester felt a rush of affection at the simple sign of sisterly love. They had grown much closer since Hester's father's visit. Sarah was standing behind Samuel and had Henry gripped in her arms. He was fussing, trying to wriggle free, having recently learned to walk. There were a few faces Hester did not recognise, and she assumed they were Adam's uncles and aunts. One woman crossed her hands over her heart; another gave a gentle approving nod. Every face showed kindness and joy and put Hester at ease.

The magistrate cleared his throat. Hester and Adam turned to face each other.

'I never thought this would happen to me,' Hester whispered to Adam.

'I was certain it would,' he whispered in return.

Hester felt her heart swell as Adam reached for her

hands. As they squeezed each other's fingers, a bulge appeared in Adam's waistcoat. Hester stifled a giggle. Adam had smuggled Shadow to their nuptial ceremony.

'In the presence of God and all witnesses present, do you, Adam Phillips, take Hester Trelawney to be your wife?'

The severe tone of the magistrate's voice reminded Hester of the solemnity of the occasion and the commitment that she and Adam were making to each other. She held her breath, waiting for Adam to answer.

Adam's eyes seemed to sparkle as he said 'I do.'

'In the presence of God and all witnesses present, do you, Hester Trelawney, accept Adam Phillips to be your husband?'

Hester could not suppress her smile. 'I do,' she replied, her voice clear and sincere.

The magistrate looked from Adam to Hester and then to the gathered witnesses. 'It is my pleasure to pronounce that Adam and Hester are now man and wife.'

A ripple of polite applause crept through the parlour. The magistrate gathered his hat and walking cane and prepared to leave the house. 'I will take my leave now and trust you will all enjoy a quiet celebration.' He stopped beside Adam. 'I must add the details of your marriage to the Court Orders.'

Hester and Adam remained where they were, having eyes only for each other.

Hester's heartbeat fluttered in her chest like the beat of a hummingbird's wings. Adam's grasp felt warm and safe as he continued to hold her hands. 'My heart is yours until I die,' she said.

She heard a catch in Adam's voice when he replied, 'And mine is yours, forever.'

Pa ushered the magistrate from the house and then approached the newlyweds. He placed one hand on Hester's shoulder and the other on Adam's. 'Congratulations,' he said to them both. 'Let us celebrate your union with a jug or two of Bride Ale.'

Adam chuckled. 'I am a little parched.'

'And our guests will be ready to feast.' Ma kissed Hester on each cheek.

Hester's appetite had deserted her. She forced herself to eat a baked clam and to swallow a mouthful of rabbit poached in beer. She nibbled a small slice of the bride cake Martha had baked, while revelling in the compliments and good wishes of every guest.

Once the guests had eaten their fill, Adam called for everyone's attention.

'My wife and I,' he said, grinning at Hester, 'thank you all for coming here today to witness and celebrate our marriage. We also thank you for your generous gifts.' He gestured towards Pa's writing table, which Ma had dragged into the parlour. An array of items covered the surface: pewter plates; a skillet; a cauldron; a miniature basket containing scissors, sewing needles and different coloured threads; a leather roll containing a mixture of small tools; and a set of knives and spoons. John and Priscilla Alden had arrived with a cart bearing two chairs. John had made the chairs himself and carved smooth, elegant arms. Priscilla had made plump cushions and embroidered them with colourful flowers. Their children had made little scented bags fragranced with dried rose petals and lavender. Adam beckoned Hester to join him. 'It's my turn to give my wife a gift.'

Hester felt her cheeks pale. She had no gift for Adam.

'I'll take this,' Ma said, relieving Hester of her stick.

Hester hobbled across the room to return to Adam's side. Adam nodded at his brother, and Hester's muscles tensed. His brother was holding a fiddle. Hester's throat dried. She shook her head at Adam. 'I can't dance,' she said.

Adam drew her closer to him and whispered in her ear. 'Yes you can, Hester. You might not jump and dart like a deer, but you can move your legs and feet. My brother has created a slower tune for his fiddle especially for this moment. I will support you as we move across the floor. Don't worry about a thing. Just follow my lead.' Adam put his hands on Hester's waist. 'Rest your hands on my shoulders.' As soon as Hester did so, his brother raised the bow to the fiddle, leaving Hester no more time to object.

The pressure of Adam's hands increased as Hester moved her right foot to the side, mirroring his step. When her left foot struck the ground, Adam took her weight. Soon, she was gliding around the room, feeling each note from the fiddle's strings in every one of her bones.

A soft warm breeze caressed Hester's cheeks as she floated through the air, giddy with joy at moving to music and safe in Adam's strong pair of hands. As Adam whirled her in a circle, she felt as free as any bird soaring high above the land without a care in the world. When the tune reached its end, Adam pulled her into an embrace.

'I will remember that dance for the rest of my life,' Hester said, choked with joy and disbelief. 'There is nothing you could have given me that would have made a better gift.'

Adam released her and bowed. 'May I have the pleasure of the second dance, too?'

'You may.' Hester giggled and added, 'And the third and fourth and fifth.'

The fiddle struck up another tune, and the guests joined them in their dance.

After the daylight faded and candles illuminated the room, Pa called a halt to the music. 'It's time for this merriment to end,' he said. 'The bride and groom must leave us now and begin their married life.'

Ma passed Hester her walking stick.

Adam stroked her cheek. 'Let the moonlight guide us home, my love, where we will retire to our marital bed.'

Everyone clapped and cheered as Hester and Adam stepped out of the house. Hester felt a surge of love for Ma and Pa as they took their turns to say farewell. She embraced her brother and sister and then kissed baby Hope's little forehead. 'I'll be back for you soon, my angel,' she said.

'Mistress Phillips.' Adam stood with his arm extended, ready for Hester to hold.

'Master Phillips,' she said, linking her arm through his. A shiver of nervous excitement passed through her as she contemplated the night ahead. Adam's mother had given them her bedchamber to use until they had a home of their own, and, for the next three nights, they would have the house to themselves while Adam's mother and younger brother stayed at his sister's house.

Hester glanced back into the room of well-wishers and

her beaming mother-in-law. She wiggled her fingers to wave farewell before walking away with Adam. Her body fizzed with happiness and her heart swelled with joy.

'This is what it means to love,' she said. 'This is what it means to belong.'

CHAPTER 38

OVER THE COURSE of the following year, Hester watched a plot of land behind the forge evolve into a house. Adam and his brother used every spare moment to hammer nails into rising clapboard walls and cover the roof with thatch. Pa and Samuel had worked the ground beyond, clearing rubble from the soil and hoeing the earth ready for Hester to plant vegetables and herbs. Ma and Martha had spent many an hour working in Ma's stillroom creating soaps, liniments, oils and balms ready for Hester to use at home or for her labouring mothers. Meanwhile, Hester and Adam's mother had strained their eyes by candlelight stitching coverlets, curtains and cushions. Now, at last, it was time to move in and turn the house into a home.

Butterflies fluttered in Hester's stomach as she walked alongside Adam. He was pushing a handcart laden with many different items: cauldrons; skillets; knives; fire irons; wooden trenchers; pewter plates; and his armour breastplate, helmet and musket. The wheels creaked as they kicked up dirt, and the cart rattled over stones. Metal clanged against metal as if beating out a tune. Ma and Pa followed with a horse and cart stacked with chests and trunks filled with clothes, furniture and linens. Martha and Adam's mother sat on the back of the cart. Martha had Hope asleep in her arms while Adam's mother gripped the handle of a large wicker basket containing packages of food for dinner and sweating jugs of ale. Samuel perched on a barrel, singing at the top of his voice and feeding Shadow walnuts.

Adam drew his handcart to a halt and wrapped an arm around Hester. 'Here we are, my darling,' he said. 'The new Phillips homestead.'

Hester kissed him on the cheek and gazed at the building. It was two storeys tall, had a central door and four windows facing towards her. The smell of warm timber permeated the air and tickled her nostrils. The thatched roof seemed to glow golden in the sunlight, and at each end of it perched a chimney, one for the kitchen hearth, the other for the parlour fire.

'It's perfect,' Hester said. 'God bless us and this house. May we be very happy living here.'

Adam gestured for Hester to approach the front door. 'After you, my lady,' he said, plunging into a deep bow.

'Arise, Sir Adam.' Hester chuckled as she pretended to knight Adam with her walking stick. She glanced beyond Adam to catch Ma beaming at them both. 'Let us unload the carts,' Hester said, 'and then share our first family meal.'

Hester and Ma hung the drapes while Adam and Pa built the bedstead. Martha arranged the table and chairs and arranged Hester's pewter ware on the dresser. Hester tasked Samuel with laying the table and setting out the food for the meal. She watched him sneak morsels of cheese for himself and feed a hazelnut to Shadow. Samuel saw Hester watching him and flushed to the roots of his hair. Hester shook her head with mock annoyance before breaking into a smile.

Adam called down the stairs, 'Hester, we're ready for you to inspect our work.'

Hester climbed the stairs using her walking stick and the handrail. Adam had asked the carpenter to build a special staircase. It turned into a partial spiral and had wide, shallow steps that made it easier for Hester to climb them. When she entered the bedchamber, she made a little gasp. The bedstead was large, with carved newel posts adorned with birds and squirrels, and there was a plump mattress. Hester pressed the mattress and raised an enquiring eyebrow at Adam.

'It's filled with horsehair and feathers,' he said. He gave Hester a boyish grin. 'Were you expecting a thin one of straw?'

Hester gave him a playful punch on the arm before moving towards the open window. She could see the sea in the distance. It was a deep shade of sapphire blue with glittering silver shimmers. A few fishing boats were making their way home after long hours on the ocean. Gulls wheeled in the air above the boats, squawking to one another. A soft breeze caught the trees nearby, rustling the leaves that would soon change colour with autumn. Hester closed her eyes and felt the air wash over her cheeks. To think she had almost lost this life to a grim future in London. Now, she had a brighter future filled with love, optimism and contentment. She was married to a man who loved her and whom she loved in return. They would raise children together and watch them flourish into adults. She would give them the comfort and encouragement she had enjoyed in her childhood with Ma and Pa. The only regret she harboured was that Ma and Pa had tried to conceal the truth about her birth. She vowed not to do the same to Hope. As soon as Hope learned to talk, she would tell her how special she was. And if the day should arrive when Hope yearned to meet her own people, Hester would do whatever she could to encourage her and help her.

'You haven't seen the other chamber yet,' Adam said, interrupting Hester's reverie and taking her hand in his. 'Close your eyes while I lead you to the door.' Hester did as she was told and took a few confident steps with Adam as her guide. After they crossed the landing, he said, 'Open your eyes!'

The sight took Hester's breath away. A small truckle bed was set against a wall and faced the chamber window. There was a large trunk carved with wild animals and another carved with flowers. 'Gifts from my uncle,' Adam said, stepping forward to lift the lids. 'One is for poppets and trinkets; the other is for clothes and shoes.'

Hester felt her eyes mist at such a generous gesture. Adam returned to her side and draped his arm around her. 'It's a chamber for Hope when she's older. I know you're not ready to put her in a room of her own, but you'll know when the time is right.'

Hope was already a year old, but Hester felt a powerful

urge to protect her, and she loved to watch her sleeping in her cot and listen to her dainty snores.

Adam planted a kiss on Hester's cheek. 'There's plenty of space for another bed or two for other children that might join us.' Adam turned Hester towards him and pulled her into an embrace. 'Are you happy?' he said, looking deep into her eyes.

Hester's skin tingled. 'More than you can imagine,' she said before pressing her lips to his.

CHAPTER 39

PLIMOTH, 1650

'Hester Trelawney?' An unfamiliar man peered over the fence next to where Hester was tending to her kitchen garden. She was clearing weeds from a herb bed while Hope played with her favourite poppet in the shade of a young cherry tree.

Hester reached for her walking stick and pushed herself up from her knees. She brushed soil dust from her skirt and used her apron to blot her brow.

'I'm Hester Phillips now,' she said, taking in the smart cut of the man's jacket and the fine quality of the cloth. He was holding the hand of a sullen little boy who was wearing clothes that were too small for him and a scruffy pair of shoes. 'How may I help you?'

The man withdrew a letter from his jacket and passed it over the fence. Hester inspected the handwriting. The letters were untidy, and the writer had smudged the ink. There was no seal on the letter, and the folds were uneven. She rested her walking stick against the fence and opened the letter. An icy chill rushed through her. The signature was Thomas Twisselton's.

Hester stared at the scrawl across the page. It looked as if her father had written in a hurry. She took her time to read each word and make sense of the scruffy writing.

Hester,

I have lost another wife since returning to England. God saw fit to punish me for failing to treat her right. My poor Alice died in childbirth, taking the babe with her. This news will not surprise you, but I swear it wasn't my fault. After Alice died, I did not cope well and sought solace in wine and dice. I frittered away my business and almost lost my house.

I know I'm not the best of men, and I want to make amends. So, I've sold my house, settled all my debts, and I'm putting my violence to good use – I have joined Cromwell's army in his fight against the Scots.

I know I have been a poor husband and father, so I am sending this request.

Please care for my son, your half-brother, and give him the life he deserves. I sent young Bartholomew to New England with my solicitor, Master Lawly. I know you'll grow to love my little boy more than I ever could.

Believe me when I tell you I want the best for all my children, and God willing, if I ever see you all again, you'll find me a better man.

Thomas Twisselton

Hester folded the letter and studied the little boy holding the solicitor's hand. He looked in need of a decent meal, a wash and a new set of clothes. 'This is Bartholomew?'

'It is.' The solicitor yanked the boy's arm to make him look up at Hester.

Hester tensed at the unnecessary roughness. 'How old is he?'

'Almost three, I think.'

The little boy cast a shy glance in Hester's direction. His eyes were the same dark brown as hers, and his cheeks were pale with scattered freckles.

'Lift him over the fence,' Hester said.

'You'll take him?'

'I will.'

Master Lawly raised an eyebrow. 'Shouldn't you ask your husband first?'

'My husband is a generous man. He would not turn away a child.'

Master Lawly lifted Bartholomew and placed him in Hester's arms. The little boy felt light for his age, in need of a good meal or two and desperate for family love. Hester smiled at Bartholomew and received a flickering movement of his lips in return. 'I am your sister, Bartholomew. And my home is your home now.'

Master Lawly had a leather bag slung across his body. He reached inside and pulled out a bulging leather purse. 'This is a down payment for your trouble. I'll have the rest brought to you from the ship. There's a small coffer filled with similar purses containing the proceeds from the sale of your father's house. A little under eighty pounds, in fact.' His sharp demeanour seemed to soften. 'It's not the fortune I had hoped to bring you. I had to pay your father's creditors first.'

'Of course you did.' Hester shifted Bartholomew in her arms. Eighty pounds might not be a fortune, but it was a sizeable sum. It would take Adam almost three years to earn the same amount.

Master Lawly adjusted the brim of his hat and bid Hester a cheery farewell. She watched the solicitor turn and walk away, his receding figure fading in the evening light.

'Who's that, Mama?' Hope cried, running towards Hester and standing on tiptoe to look at Bartholomew.

Hester stroked Hope's glossy dark curls. 'This is my little brother, sweeting. He lives with us now.'

Hester lowered Bartholomew to the ground. Hope

reached for his hand. 'We have puppies, Bartholomew. Would you like to see them?'

Hester watched Hope lead Bartholomew towards the barn, where their spaniel was nursing her pups. The dog was another of Adam's rescues after he found her with her leg in a trap. Hester weighed the purse in her hand and thought about the purses on the ship. Eighty pounds would be enough to buy a larger house. They would need it for all the animals Adam had rescued. They would need it for the children yet to come.

'Hester?' Adam's voice made her reach for her stick and hurry towards the house. When she reached the door to the kitchen, he wrapped her in his arms. 'We have exciting news. Do you want to tell her, William?'

William's cheeks flushed to the roots of his curly flaxen hair. He had joined the household two years earlier after his parents died in a fire. Eleven years old, shy and awkward, he had not spoken a word for the first three months, but Adam's kind manner and Hester's love had helped him come back to himself.

'You won't believe it, Ma,' William said grinning, 'but someone's offered Pa an opportunity to buy a forge in Boston!'

Hester raised her eyebrows. 'Are you tempted to do it?'

Adam removed his cap and twisted it in his hands. 'There's not enough work here for both my brother and me, and it's a dream of an opportunity. It would offer a fine future for young William here, and a comfortable living for us. It might be a struggle while I build my reputation, but I know we can get by. Boston needs its first farrier, and I would love to fill that role.' Adam appeared concerned by her lack of reaction. 'If you're worried about how we would pay for it, I have already negotiated an agreement. The blacksmith is happy for me to pay him in instalments over the next eight years.' He furrowed his brow. 'We needn't move if you'd rather stay here. We're comfortable enough as we are.'

Hester considered their growing family and the opportunities Boston would offer. 'I think it's a good idea,' she said. 'And I think you should buy the forge.' To William she said, 'Will you check on Hope for me? She's in the barn with the puppies, and she has a surprise for you.'

As soon as William was out of earshot, Hester told Adam about Master Lawly's visit. 'It will help with the costs of moving to Boston and give us any money we need while you build up your business.' She glanced towards their home. 'We will need a house larger than this now that my brother has joined our family.'

'Another little boy,' Adam said, with a wondrous expression. 'The Lord blesses us again.'

'Papa! Papa!' Hope came running out of the barn and charged across the yard, her skirt threatening to bind her legs and drag her to the ground. 'Papa, look!' She pointed back towards the barn, where William was leading Bartholomew by the hand. 'We have a new brother!'

Hester looked at Adam and her children and felt a surge of contentment. This was who she was. A faithful wife and a doting mother. A beloved daughter and a midwife. She was Hester Phillips now, the Trelawney girl that was. 'I think it's time we had something to eat,' she said. 'Who here is hungry?'

'Me!' squealed Hope. 'And Barty too.'

Hester smiled at the fondness Hope had already nurtured for Bartholomew.

'I could eat a whole pig,' William said, making Hope roll her eyes in pretend annoyance.

'You'll have to fight me for it,' Adam said. He swept Bartholomew off his feet and twirled him round in a circle. The little boy's face seemed to light up, and he asked Adam to spin him again. Adam grinned and said, 'After I've danced with your sister.'

Laughing, Hester allowed Adam to pass her walking stick to Hope before he swept her off her feet. He hummed a tune so close to her ear that she could feel his warm breath. She revelled in Adam's firm touch as he led her in circles around the yard. All the while he supported her weight, allowing her to feel the joy of the movement and a gentle breeze on her face.

'Dance, Mama! Dance!' Hope placed Hester's stick on the ground and eagerly clapped her hands.

'Dance!' Bartholomew shouted, clapping along with her and then grasping Hope's wrists. 'Dance!'

'Look at William,' Hester said to Adam, when he put her down.

William was leading a circular jig with Hope and Bartholomew following his lead and squealing with laughter.

'Can we eat now, Ma?' William brought the jig to a halt. He bent forward with his hands on his hips, gasping for breath.

'I think that's a good idea,' Hester said, admiring the flushed faces of her children. 'Wash your hands and set the table. Supper will be ready in a few minutes.'

Bacon sizzled on the skillet, its scent making Hester's mouth water. Adam bounced Bartholomew on his lap, then tickled him under the chin, drawing a torrent of giggles. Hester smiled. These children had a loving home and doting parents, related by blood or not. She had her own family to love and nurture, and a future beckoning in Boston. She cracked an egg onto the skillet and let out a soft gasp.

'Hester?' Adam's eyes widened with concern. 'Did you burn yourself?'

'No, dearest. It's nothing to worry about.' Hester beamed at her handsome, loving husband with his halo of shimmering orange curls. 'In fact, I have joyful news to share.' She rested her palms on the soft swell of her belly. 'I felt a flutter inside my womb. I believe I am with child.'

THE END

THANK YOU FOR READING THIS BOOK.

I hope you enjoyed reading this tale about Hester. If you did, and you can spare a minute or two, it would mean the world to me if you would leave an honest review on your favourite bookstore's website.

Now that you have finished this novel, you might enjoy my other books:

The Second Mrs Thistlewood

The Roseland Collection
Mawde of Roseland
Mistress of Carrick

The Mayflower Collection
Winds of Change
Running With The Wind
The Winter Years

You might also like to subscribe to my newsletter

My monthly newsletter includes updates about my novels, short articles that I think will be of interest to you, advance notification of my new releases, discounts and other offers. You will receive a FREE downloadable novella when you subscribe. I'll never pass on your information to third parties, and you can unsubscribe at any time. If you would like to receive my monthly updates or learn more about me and my other published books, please visit my website at www.dionnehaynes.com.

SELECT BIBLIOGRAPHY

I read many books and articles before writing this story, but here is a short selection that might be of interest to you:

Mayflower by Nathaniel Philbrick

On The Trail Of The Pilgrim Fathers by J. Keith Cheetham

Everyday Life in the Massachusetts Bay Colony by George Francis Dow

www.colonialsociety.org (Colonial Society of Massachusetts)

www.plimoth.org (the website for the Plimoth Patuxet Museums)

ACKNOWLEDGMENTS

Thank you, Kristina Stanley and the editors at Fictionary. I have learned so much from you about the important elements needed to make a story work, and the live classes have turned structural editing into a writing task that is fun!

Thank you, Bev (superscriptproofreading.co.uk), for your meticulous attention to detail and for polishing my work so well.

Thank you, Dee Dee (www.deedeebookcovers.com), for a beautiful cover design that captures the essence of this tale.

Thank you to my family and friends for your unwavering love and support.

Thank you, Paul, for everything. You mean the world to me.

www.ingramcontent.com/pod-product-compliance
Lightning Source LLC
LaVergne TN
LVHW040304121125
825532LV00013B/452